An Uneven Step

Can love be lost if enmity rules?

– KATHLEEN STEELE –

An environmentally friendly book printed and bound in England by
www.printondemand-worldwide.com

www.fast-print.net/store.php

An Uneven Step
Copyright © Kathleen Steele 2011

ISBN 978-178035-056-1

First published 2011 by
FASTPRINT PUBLISHING
Peterborough, England.

Acknowledgements

My thanks to all those who have contributed in the compilation of this story.

Chapter One

It was dark when Josie Craven finally arrived at the place so the puzzle remained as to why she had ventured out onto the promenade to cast her eyes at the sea in the first place. This apparently appeared to be something to which she could find little answer, unless it rebounded from sheer frustration at not being able to continue on her journey until the following day, for all she could now actually visualise in that dusky grey were the lights of the pier, shining forth as if they were in denial that the end of the season had passed and equally determined that if they made the effort to keep shining then they would eventually attract the visitors back again to the place.

Maybe in all truth she had craved for the familiar ozone to fill her lungs as well as the salt from the waves that pounded the shore to tingle against her cheeks again. Perhaps indeed she had longed for the place where the seagulls squawked and surfed the waves of the on coming tide that awaited the stiff breeze to decide its part in the instilling of a roaring momentum. Even so such memories that now occurred were from days in the distant past, a time when she herself had been carefree and devoid of worry. It had also happened in a far different part of the country to where she was now. But at this time of the day few cars ventured to stop along that promenade and satiate their passengers with the view. Indeed the only vehicles that passed along the whole stretch all appeared to be in a hurry to get somewhere and thus the drivers of such vehicles felt that they had little time to loiter.

All of this of course was apart from one solitary vehicle that appeared to be black in the darkness of the night and Josie watched with not a little curiosity as its driver decided to alight from the comfort of his shell. It seemed to her to be surprising too that the man appeared to be on his own for to all intent and purposes he appeared to be young and well dressed, and yet upon reflection she also noticed that there was a look of determination set within his features that gave his jaw the appearance of being chisel shaped.

Perhaps he must have sensed that someone was looking at him for he glanced across the road and probably because she was the only person who had ventured out onto the promenade at that time, providing that one discarded the presence of the wino who had taken to the bushes to consume his bottle, he nodded in her direction, mounted the steps that led into a nearby building and was gone as quickly as he had appeared. The fact was that his purposeful stride made Josie think yet again about her own mission, for she was destined to be here for only a short time for tomorrow she would be making her way to catch the night ferry and heading towards her predestined meeting, the one that she had been cajoled into!

In one sense this was a journey she would much preferred not to have taken but she reminded herself in the severest of tones that it was after all her duty to be going. For after all this was something that she owed to her father after his life had found an early termination, and the powers that be had not been too reticent to reinforce her own conscious and remind her of a debt that she owed to him. This of course was her sole reason for being here, not to smell the ozone no matter what memories it evoked, and certainly not to taste the salt upon her lips, but rather to catch the boat that left from the port that was not too far distant.

The documentation that she needed was currently resting in her hand luggage and because she had undertaken this mission the boffins had even thrown in a few hundred Euros to cover any additional expenditure she might incur. Thus she had to content herself with the fact that perhaps before too much time had elapsed she would be arriving in Rotterdam before travelling on to meet her contact in a place in a specified location in the Loreley valley along the Rhine.

"Have you got a light Miss?" She hadn't noticed the teenager until the voice broke into her trend of thought and shaking her head in denial Josie glanced down at the wisp of a child who had served to interrupt her thoughts. She shook her head and was in half a mind to tell the teenager that she was far too young to become addicted to this filthy habit, when the girl, peering more closely at her suddenly burst forth with a song of recognition. "Here aren't you that Josie Craven who is on the tele?"

Josie felt forced to smile as she half nodded to the girl whilst not really wanting to be drawn into further conversation but refusing to be pointedly rude by ignoring the child, for after all she had been young herself, both young and naive come to that, but someone who had the freedom to be able to take off on those shifting sands to enjoy exploring the various nooks and crannies of mystery that each tide managed to reveal and what was more to have no one she had to answer to for these indulgencies.

"Tell me, did you really fire that gun when you arrested those smugglers?" The child was still persistent in her questioning and perhaps because she was curious and demanded an answer Josie nodded yet again. "Cor blimey, but where did you learn to shoot like that Miss?"

"I'm afraid you shouldn't always believe what you can see on the screen and regard it as gospel!" Josie found her hands straying to the weapon that she currently wore, the one that she was trying hard to forget about.

"That's what my dad says, but then he has never met you, am I right?"

"I expect you are right!" Now Josie looked for a way out of this situation. In truth the child meant well but Josie certainly did not desire to carry on with this conversation any longer than was absolutely necessary. Therefore with this in mind she needed to get away but without being totally rude to the child. It was perhaps fortuitous that at the time she caught a glimpse of the figure of the man now leaving the building he had previously entered in something of a hurry and it was almost without a second thought that she shouted out in his direction.

"Ah there you are! A girl can easily catch a cold waiting around like this for you. Did the business go O.K. in there?"

The man looked at her nonplus for a moment and then sensing that this must have something to do with the child, he suddenly smiled, an expression that served to light up his features. "Extremely satisfactory I would say. Now what was it you said earlier about us having a drink?" He linked his arm with her own as if indicating that the two knew each other well, and although she was surprised at this action it did at least get rid of the girl who disappeared murmuring something about adults and their mannerisms. Still Josie was even more surprised when with their arms still firmly entwined the stranger escorted her into a nearby bar. "So what will you have then? Oh dear I forgot we haven't introduced ourselves yet. I am Gregg Anderson by the way and you are----?"

"Josie ---Josie Craven!" Her voice sounded flat as she echoed the words.

"Otherwise known of as Kimberley Clark if one well known soap opera on our television screen is to be believed!" So he had recognised her as well. The thought of this made her groan for it was certainly something she wanted to get away from at this time.

"I prefer to forget about that when I am away from the set if you don't mind!"

"But you can't disguise your face. Why even your fan club recognised you! Anyway what are you having to drink if you wish to forget about your fame?"

"In that case just a lime and lemon please!" He raised his eyebrows as if he had been expecting her choice to be a little more exotic, but then snapped his fingers for the waiter to come running in attendance without further ado! "And mine is a lager without anything added!" She thought his look as he passed the order to be meaningful. But surely that was the trouble for she appeared to be reading things into everything nowadays, especially since she had been apportioned this challenge! "So what part of the country do you spring from? I can tell by your accent that you are not from these parts!"

"No as a matter of fact I am just passing through, I was actually born and raised on the other coast!" She decided that this was enough information for she most certainly did not want to divulge what she was doing here now.

"So are you here on holiday or what?" The man appeared to be persistent.

"No, as I said I am merely passing through. As a matter of fact I am only staying here over night before I head for the night ferry tomorrow. I'm afraid that I couldn't get a berth before then. Hence you have the lamentable sight of one deranged female wandering along the promenade at this hour when she ought to be occupied in doing something more practical. A factor that you yourself have just witnessed!"

"I can't agree with that! So you are heading to Rotterdam then?" The man obviously knew his sailings.

Josie suddenly didn't want to think anymore for a night cooped up in an inside cabin did little to placate her equilibrium: And for what? She demanded the answer from herself but received no response to her question. It was time for her to try to change the subject. "But what of you yourself? I must say that you are looking very prosperous Gregg dressed in that manner. Are you here on business?" She thought now of him visiting that property.

"Sort of, I suppose you could say that but there again prosperity does not come into it!" He appeared to be a little tight lipped and was obviously not for explaining anymore. He sought to change the subject. "So where are you staying whilst you are so called passing through?"

"At the Devonshire overnight!"

"Quite a nice place the Devonshire I believe. But has nobody there recognised the face from off their television screens?"

"Hardly! I don't really think the sort of television that I appear in is particularly sought after by the geriatric set! After all it is supposed to be for children, damn it!"

"Well I suppose your geriatrics could have grandchildren!"

"Gregg, can we please forget about television. That is what I am currently trying to do and I don't need reminding of my role either!"

"Fair enough!" He shrugged his shoulders. "So instead tell me what you are going to do in Rotterdam?"

"Actually I am not going to do anything, for once I arrive there I shall be catching a coach to Koblenz where I am due to meet someone!"

"A boy friend? Confound it, why is it that when I find myself an attractive girl then she is already spoken for?"

"Not a boy friend no! Actually it is someone that I need to pass a message onto!" She was conscious yet again of the weapon pressing against her flesh

"Methinks the lady gets more and more mysterious. I wonder whether in the television world she inhabits they have ever heard of telephones to pass on messages?"

"Gregg; I am afraid this matter is personal!"

"Sorry!" He held up his hands. "Trust Gregg Anderson to get hold of the wrong end of the stick!"

He said no more. Perhaps in all truth he was still waiting for Josie to enlighten him, but that was a something that she could not do. Therefore they finished their drinks and then parted, Gregg taking her by the hand and pressing it firmly. "It has been very interesting meeting you anyway Josie. As a matter of fact I had always wondered what television stars were like in real life!"

She let him go at that before she realised that she had not discovered what he was doing here himself.

The strange sequel to the matter appeared that she was going to be afforded that opportunity sooner than she could have anticipated. After boarding the boat the following day and suffering the indignity of having to hump her case up four flights of stairs to reach the embarkation deck just because she had a dread of escalators, Josie decided to go for her evening meal early before the restaurant got typically crowded with those who demanded their sustenance at an appointed hour. Even so the table she had eyed that was tucked away in a corner of the place where few could see her was not destined to be her lot, for even as she waited for the maitre to permit the opening of this dining room she sensed his presence right behind her, and turning her head found that her senses had not been deceiving her.

"So we meet again Miss Craven!"

"But you never said!" Josie cast him an accusing glance as if this was indeed a mortal sin.

"Come to think of it you never asked!" His lips curled and for a moment she wondered whether he was being sarcastic. "Oh come off it Josie. As we happen to be here together, number one and number two in the queue so as to speak we might as well share a table. That way we will make far less work for the staff here! Perhaps after all it is as well to eat whilst we are still in port!"

His words were blatantly obvious and for a moment she wondered whether he had set himself out to be some sort of Job's comforter, for the wind that had been so refreshing when she had been sat out on the promenade the previous night had seemingly quickened in its pace. She supposed she should have realised the possibility of a rough sail when the gantry had been declared out of commission and folk had been forced to board by the car decks a factor that had caused sheer mayhem if one desired a lift up to the appropriate deck. Therefore in all truth she didn't really require him to remind her by behaving as if he was some superior intellect in the matter.

Still he now gave her little option to object for the doors were currently opening and the headwaiter took them as being a couple. Nor had Gregg finished for no sooner had he clapped his eyes on the wine waiter that he ordered a bottle of wine from the list.

"I don't drink-----!" She still tried to object as her glass was being filled.

"Just remember that you don't have to drive anywhere tonight, neither do you have to find your accommodation in that resort, so why not sit back and enjoy yourself for once?" He almost dared her with his eyes to place the glass to her lips. The liquid smelt strangely refreshing, almost like it had that other time, which was now so long ago. But then she determined that there was no way that Gregg Anderson was going to see her relaxed.

"I'll go and collect my dinner!" The restaurant operating on self service lines almost provided an answer to her prayers for it gave her time to think and in all truth the appearance of this man on the boat was too much of a coincidence for her to swallow!

By the time they had finished the meal however the movement of the boat now that it had left port had become quite apparent and Gregg regarded her with not a little concern.

"Had you anything planned for tonight?"

She shook her head with some vigour for even if she had anything planned she determined that there was no way that she was going to confide in this stranger. "No, I thought I would have an early night considering the hour having to be put onto the clock and also being forced to make an early rise in the morning. As well as that I also need to prepare for the long coach journey that lies in front of me tomorrow!"

"In that case you had better allow me the privilege of seeing you to your cabin!" He stood, frowning a little as he weighed up the sudden squall that was causing the boat to toss.

"I can assure you that I will be perfectly all right!" Perhaps however this was something of an understatement for the boat giving a sudden pitch made her reach out to grab a handrail for support.

"Well in that case have it your own way then!" There was a positive gleam in the man's eye as he uttered the words almost as if he expected to see her doing a right purler in front of him.

Life as far as Josie Craven was concerned appeared to be quite straight forward as she passed her school learning years and had then gone on to University in a veiled attempt to study law. It was straight forward in one sense yet disappointing in another for after starring in several dramatic productions whilst she was at school Josie would have dearly have loved to have followed a dramatic arts career along with some of the friends she had made but at the time her parents and especially her father would hear nothing of it!

"Stop talking rubbish girl and get yourself a worthwhile career with those brains you've inherited!" That of course had been her father's comments when he had been on leave from the Services. Funny she had not known at the time what he did there, but her mother had informed her that he was in Intelligence. He had never known that when she did go to University she had chosen drama as a subsidiary subject in her degree, which was just as well, for Josie had found she could not cope with the rigours of the law course. She had often wondered whether if she had initially chosen some other discipline things might have been different. For starters she would probably have never met Paul Butler. It wasn't that the two of them were attracted for Josie had already made up her mind that she needed to study and thus she had wanted no entanglements. Paul also had been a serious faced academic with little time for any romantic dalliances. Yet now their lives appeared to be intrinsically linked because of her father for despite her mother's reassurance that he worked for army Intelligence she had never in a million years guessed whom the man was really working for! Not that was until one day a serious faced individual had appeared on the doorstep to impart the news and by that time Josie, after her mother's untimely death with breast cancer had, without consulting her father, forgone her proposed career in law and found herself a part in children's television.

" I am afraid that I have to inform you that your father has been seriously hurt whilst in action but we trust that in time that we will be able to get him back to this country. But you are on television, am I right Miss Craven?"

She had a guilt complex because her father had been out of the country when she had flunked those law examinations and therefore he had not been there to pull his face and try to stop her from following her chosen career and whether it was because she was photogenic or not she had found surprisingly little difficulty in being noticed by those television boffins and in a very short space of time she had been offered a role in a brand new production. Initially the producers had presumed that it would last for a mere six weeks, which was why an unknown had been offered the part, but instead the series has become a favourite in children's viewing and had stayed to dominate the screen.

"I am yes, but please tell me more about my father. I know that he has been away from home for some time but I have no idea what he was supposed to be doing. Where is he now and what has happened to him?"

"He was serving his country Miss Craven, surely you were aware of that!"

"Then if he is injured then I must go to him!"

"I am sorry but that is quite impossible. The business happens to be a Service matter!"

"Service, what Service are we talking about?" Something in the tone of her voice must have alerted her caller.

"You really have no idea have you Miss Craven?" Perhaps she had exuded sympathy from him but this was something that she certainly did not want.

"No, but I am going to make damned sure I find out!" Her caller looked a little perplexed. He had realised previously that this call was going to prove difficult but no one had thought to inform him that he would have to face such a protagonist. "If you can't help me then please find me someone who can!"

"I promise that I will see what I can do. Perhaps if you formally requested an appointment with my superior-----!"

"Damn your appointment system. You come here to tell me that my father has been seriously injured and then tell me to make an appointment to see someone? I have already said that if my father is injured then I wish to go to him, so you now know exactly what you can do with your appointment system. Tell me now exactly where my father is!"

"Look I will speak to someone and then contact you in return!" He made his escape before she could resist anymore. Strangely enough, whether it was because the guy was worried what she might do or otherwise he did manage to phone her the next day with an invite to see someone in the city.

The fact that this interfered with rehearsals counted for nothing for in some senses she still felt as if she had let her father down by not succeeding in passing that law course he had mapped out for her and therefore she was shortly to find herself in a room that was situated in some obscure part of the city facing a man who currently peered at her over his spectacles, almost indeed as if he was assessing the girl for some major role and Josie decided that if he came out with some comment about her being on television she would definitely throw something at him. It didn't come to that however for the man facing her had obviously something on his mind.

"I'm sorry to have to tell you this Miss Craven, but we have just received a call from one of our men in the field. Your father unfortunately died this morning. His injuries were life threatening but initially we had hoped to get him back to England!"

Josie felt as if the room began to shake uncontrollably around her. Her father was dead and yet she still had so much to tell him, so much to put to rights between them. "Where is he? I still wish to go to him!"

"Miss Craven I don't think that you are aware that your father was employed on a mission that involved its own dangers!"

"Mission –what are you talking about? My father was in the Services in Intelligence!"

"Quite so Miss Craven. Your father also happened to be one of our most trusted agents!"

"Agent? Agent in what?"

"You mean to tell me that you had no idea of his work even though he spent a great deal of his time out of the country?"

"I know that he was interested in old maps---it appeared to be a hobby he took up quite recently!"

"Ah maps, yes! Well I suppose one can concede that is part of the story!"

"I'm sorry to appear pedantic Sir, but perhaps you didn't hear me the first time around, I want to go to him now!"

"I'm sorry but that privilege is extended to Service personnel only for our exact location is known to only a few people!"

"In that case I will join your blasted Service. Well do you have to swear me in or something?"

The man facing her appeared to wring his hands in desperation. "I'm afraid that it is not quite as simple as that Miss Craven. You see you will require assessment, training, a medical and an aptitude test before you could even be considered for such a position as well as passing security clearance. By which time no doubt your father's remains will have been returned to this country!"

"In that case maybe I should be considered to take over my father's role out there, wherever out there happens to be?" She didn't know why her father's words of long ago about taking an uneven step suddenly occurred to her. Was this endeavour she now intended to take simply that? But then she didn't really care for now all she desired was the opportunity to try and repay her father for all his years of tutorage.

"That is quite a nonsensical argument on your part Miss Craven. Besides I believe you have your own career in this country. An actress, or so I am told!"

"A quality that no doubt I would be able to put to good use, a factor that you must agree with me on. As far as my job goes then you need not worry for I can easily get myself written out of the script for a while!"

"Whilst I must concede that your acting role could provide a useful front to other activities, maybe it is not such a good idea. But tell me in view of your father's demise, why are you still so determined to take on this job?"

"The answer to that Sir is quite simple. Maybe I believe that I owe this to my father for things that have happened between us in the past!"

"Hmmm!" The man now regarded her rather clinically as if he was about to make a final assessment. "In that case maybe, just maybe, you will be hearing from us Miss Craven and now I must ask you to excuse me!"

The call came far sooner than what she had anticipated and at the time she did wonder whether this was to do with the fact that they seemed unable to keep their agents in the upright position and therefore they had found that they were falling short of them in the field.

Still the day she was required to report for the start of her training programme, her father's funeral was over and she had managed to say her final goodbyes, swearing over the coffin that she would avenge his death in some way. At the time she had never noticed the dark impenetrable figure who had stood silently in the background and then disappeared immediately the Service had been completed for if she had she may possibly have noticed some recognisable features to the man. But then no one else in that small gathering had noticed him either and therefore it was as if this figure had never existed.

The training sessions were far from being easy and yet she probably surprised her teachers with her dogged determination to succeed as well as her aptitude and capacity to react to differing circumstances.

"My drama training of course!" At times it seemed to be easy to be able to brag about this until some weeks later she was to find herself back in that same room now being interviewed by the same man she had seen before except that this time around he had a wad of papers in front of him that he appeared to be going through quite meticulously.

"Your training appeared to go well Miss Craven and your handling of weapons excellent according to this report. But there is still one thing however that perhaps we have not touched upon yet. The fact is whether you realise that in this profession you might be actually called upon to use these in order to kill a man?"

"I appear to have been doing that every day on television Sir!"

"But this is for real. No more bang-bang you're dead scenarios for we are not talking about the celluloid version!"

"Thinking in terms of avenging my father's death I don't consider I would find any difficulty in doing that Sir!"

"I understand that you attended University with a Paul Butler?"

"I knew him yes, not intimately for the man never chose to mix!"

"He had good reason. You said, and I quote that you wanted to find your father's killer/ Well if that is still the case then you do not have to look much farther. We believe the suspect is currently in the Rhine region!"

"Why did he have cause to take my father's life?" It was still painful for her to ask such a question but nevertheless it was something that her heart demanded to know.

"We have reason to believe that his employers are currently in the process of trying to undermine a certain expedition that is due to take place shortly. An expedition that could in the long term prove to be beneficial to our nation!"

"Let me get this straight. You want me to find this creature and to kill him?"

"If you still wish to avenge your father's death as well as winning the gratitude of our nation, the word is yes! I must stress however that you will be strictly on your own in this endeavour. If things should go wrong we will naturally deny having employed you for it would not be in the country's interest for us to become involved!"

Back in her cabin however Josie could not help but remember at least some of the conversation that had transpired. To start with the mention of Paul Butler's name had been something of a shock to her and one that she was still reeling from. For in all truth whoever would have believed that the serious minded student she had once known would have ever resorted to doing a thing like this. But it was still her father's life that she was out to avenge and if that man happened to be guilty of taking it, then however the guy had appeared at College bore no significance in what destiny had chosen for her to complete.

Still even after she had persuaded herself that she had done the right thing in returning to her cabin after the meal she found great difficulty in relaxing there. This had nothing at all to do with the crossing for the motion of the boat far from being a distraction was somehow soothing and her cabin, despite all that she had said earlier appeared to be comfy enough. She was also tired and yet any form of sleep was to avoid her like the plague and when she did finally close her eyes it was pictured of Paul Butler that appeared in front of her. Eventually possibly through sheer exhaustion she must have finally succumb for she was awakened rather hurriedly when the announcement came over the Tannoy system that they were now due to dock in Rotterdam!

The truth of the matter was that Gregg Anderson had by this time decided that he must have been definitely losing his touch. Let's face it, he had met this chick, a damned attractive one too, not merely once but also on a subsequent occasion. Yet as pleasant as the girl was she was persistent in trying to give him the big E. He glanced in the mirror that was stationed over the bar and the reflection he saw was of someone young, not too bad looking and completely eligible. What therefore was it that was wrong with him for hadn't this girl sought his companionship in the first place? He most certainly did not remember having trouble with any female like this before. He valiantly tried to bring to mind his own reason for being here as he hugged a pint to drown his sorrow. As a marine biologist he was at the time travelling to Amsterdam to meet up with a colleague and there the two of them intended to plan and prepare for a certain expedition that was close to both of their hearts. Of course what initially had been intended to be a private matter was a something that the newspaper tabloids had managed to get hold of. And of course to sell extra copy they had succeeded in spreading the so-called theory of the location of the lost city of Atlantis all over the daily papers!

The theory had been disputed of course and fortunately for the two of them there were others, ever mindful of making a quick buck, who had grabbed the opportunity to crawl out of the woodwork and claim that the lost city was situated in an entirely different place, or as it happened in several different places, and annoying as it had been at the time, Gregg had later to admit that such counter rumours had succeeded in taking some of the heat away from their own theory and quite naturally seven days after its initial publication the whole issue had been dismissed from the conscious mind of Joe Public.

Now however Helmut had decided that they had probably waited for long enough for the furore to die down and therefore this was the reason for Gregg's journey. To plan the final details with his colleague, a person whose academic qualifications Gregg admired tremendously.

He suddenly was aware of yet another person coming into that bar area and he blinked in rapid succession for this was someone he had not seen since sixth form. The last he had heard of the chap was when he had won a place to some high faluting University to study law.

"Hi Paul, remember me Gregg Anderson? We were at sixth form together!"

The other man stopped and turned and Gregg was more than a little surprised to see an icy look of contempt in the man's eyes. "I am sorry but I think that you have got the wrong person. Now if you will excuse me!"

Gregg's jaw sagged a little at the rebuff. This appeared to be his allotted reaction tonight and yet he was still convinced that this man was Paul Butler, the lad he had known at sixth form. Well he knew that this person was supposed to be supremely clever, but if this was what studying law at that place did for a bloke then you could keep it and no mistake. He would far rather take his own chances in dealing with the sea and the creatures that lived in it, thank you very much!

The turning of the windmills as the boat approached its final docking space jolted Josie's thoughts back again into reality. Sitting in the lounge and awaiting the call to disembark had appeared to her almost an imposition for now she felt she was so close to achieving her objective and yet everything now appeared to demand its rightful place in the general perspective of things. All she could in fact now hope for was that there was not the subsequent mad scramble for the lifts to transport her back to the car deck and that the gantry in this place was at lease workable.

For some obscure reason in actual fact Josie did manage to escape from the rat race quite early, possibly one reason for this being that a certain school party had settled down to block the exit on one side of the boat and whether it was for this reason the powers that be had decided that all the passengers should disembark at the opposite side of the ship. Being still extremely fit after her training Josie thus managed to secure herself a place in the first group of twenty-five allowed to leave from that large number of tourists on board. Thus having made good her own escape and believing that her connecting coach was not due to leave for some considerable time she found at least some satisfaction in sitting watching the expressions on the faces of the others as they queued patiently for the immigration control.

She watched as she saw Gregg Anderson still in that queue but it was not so much this person who riveted her attention but the one who closely followed him, the person she was supposed to be travelling up the Rhine to see. "Paul Butler!" The words formed on her lips. The man turned and glanced at her a trifle disdainfully before he moved to the passport control and after exchanging a quick word with the officials he was one person who did not appear to have to bide his time with the rest. That was when she rose to her feet in a veiled attempt to follow him.

Even so the wind appeared still determined to exact its final moment of revenge, for after almost reaching access to the car park where she trusted she would find her coach to transport her on the final leg of her journey that villain chose to blow the documentation she was already holding clean out of her hand whilst at the same time she found that the element proved strong enough to even pitch her off her feet and against a metal fence.

"Look, you're hurt!" Of course it had to be Gregg again who was the one to come to her assistance and helped her up from her unladylike position.

"I can assure you that I am perfectly all right!" In truth she desperately tried to shake herself back into the present resenting the intrusion.

"Your papers, they blew through the railings!"

Josie inwardly cursed. She had only taken the documentation out in order to establish the bus number she was supposed to catch and had never expected such a gust to have taken it clean out of her hands. In retrospect she realised she should never have been carrying it for not only did the paper contain her contacts details but also a varying set of numbers that she should have already have memorised but had not done so, but in her determination to follow the figure of Paul Butler she had forgotten all about them

"Look I'll go round and get it for you if you are sure that you are all right?" She wanted to stop him and complete the task for herself but by this time even before she had fully recovered her breath he was already on his way to have a word with the policeman to ask if he would be let through into the car lanes that lay beyond the fence and now she could only watch.

"Guess you were lucky! I didn't think he was going to let me through!" He was back again now holding the documentation up as if it was some prize trophy.

"I didn't know you knew Paul Butler?" The words were out before she could stop herself and she consoled herself that it was curiosity more than anything else that had made her ask

"Oh Paul, we went to sixth form together. Didn't know he was on the boat until I spotted him in the queue. But how did you know?"

"We actually went to University together!" She failed to explain that this had only been for a short time until she had failed her first year law examinations, but then she considered that it was none of this man's business anyway. Still at least this strange scenario proved to be enough to cause them both to break out in laughter.

"Now that I consider is much better. You have far too pretty a face than to spoil it with scowling and laughter makes it appear all the more fetching!"

"I thought you said that your friend was meeting you here?" Her words sounded ungrateful, but she was anxious to end this conversation as she grabbed hold of the documentation hoping that he had not found the opportunity to look inside.

"And I thought that you had a connection to make, that you were in something of a hurry especially after the way you left the boat?"

"I believe I must have initially miscalculated the timing!" She determined that she would give no leeway.

"More and more curious for it appears that I also have to wait for Helmut to make my connection to Amsterdam. All of which affords us some time to talk methinks!"

"Talk! What about?"

"Well we could always make a start by discussing the person you appeared anxious to spot or otherwise. You say that you once knew Paul Butler?"

Josie shook her head a little confused. "I told you I only knew him for a short time when I was at University on the same course!"

"So you were one of the boffin heads in those days too. I suppose that really doesn't surprise me!"

"I can assure you Mr Anderson that I was no boffin head as you like to term it. In all truth I suppose I was cajoled into a certain course because of pressure brought to bear by my father. But I am afraid it was never for me for in truth I found the law a load of gobbledegook. Therefore one I had flunked my first year exams I seized upon the opportunity to get out of that course and follow my true vocation in the dramatic arts. Hence my current employ in television!"

"I suppose one should express sympathy, but I have the distinct feeling that you don't want that!"

"Certainly not! But that is enough talk about me and my erstwhile career brought about because we have spotted one man!" Now she felt she needed to change the onus from off herself. "You said that you were at sixth form with the man yourself, what happened next?"

"I guess I followed my own particular interest in marine biology, not to please anyone outside of myself!"

"And that is the reason why you are currently heading towards Amsterdam?"

"I will say one thing about you Miss Craven and that is you have an insatiable curiosity. Yet on the other hand one has to agree that you are right in your assumption! Now it is your turn. What is it that the Rhine valley promises a flourishing T.V. starlet?"

"Perhaps the answer to your reasoning could be because of my father's untimely death!" She chided herself now biting on her lip as she considered she had said far too much all ready.

"You are indeed a woman of mystery!" Fortunately he did not probe further, Not that she could have revealed more for the pressure of the Official Secrets Act pressed almost as hard as the weapon she still currently wore beneath her clothing and she searched for an opportunity to get away from this man even if this meant going back to sit alone in that soulless terminal building where now most of the former passengers from off that ferry had finally departed. Perhaps it was indeed good fortune that she spotted the young man now looking in Gregg's direction.

"I think someone is trying to attract your attention!" At least it had the effect of making him turn.

"Helmut you mean? He is here already!" She glanced up as he motioned towards the young Dutchman who was already regarding her with some curiosity.

"It appears that you have had an unfortunate beginning to your visit to our country Miss. I can only say that I sincerely hope such bad luck will now leave you!" The man seemed to be friendly enough but all Josie wanted to do was to get out of this situation.

"I do believe that I have a bus to catch!" She was fumbling now and not daring to look for direction in the documentation.

"If it helps the Koblenz bus is the only long distance bus present a the moment. I believe Gregg did say that you were heading in that direction, if I might be so bold as to quote his words!"

She bit her lip. The whole business appeared to be getting far too complicated for her liking and the others were left to watch her quick departure. Helmut looked questioning at Gregg who shook his head.

"There goes one charming female I have met but as she is not going in our direction I guess our paths will not cross again!"

★ ★ ★ ★

Chapter Two

Josie Craven openly cursed. Nothing apparently was destined to go right in her life. She had passed along miles of flat uninteresting roads where one could easily have been left to ponder over things past and the task in hand. A road that had been punctuated by names that to her had previously been merely dots upon a map, whilst the ominous cloud that persisted in hanging overhead served to depress her spirits even further when she actually lost sight of the Rhine for a time.

The crossing into Germany had been hallmarked with a stud farm but now the terrain appeared to be greener and even the sun had begun to try to shine for a time. More familiar names now appeared by the roadside offering at least new hope and after passing by Cologne the countryside had become far more undulating and therefore far more interesting.

Finally the coach had dropped her by the river in Koblenz close to where those River cruise boats pulled in so that the folk on board could go ashore to view the city.

This was the place where she had expected her contact to alight, Perhaps she was still living in too much hope of meeting her contact for she had been told that he would be arriving on the River Cruiser Serenity, moored but a short distance for her to walk from the Peter Alfmeter Ufer where the coach had dropped her. Yet although she had travelled all the way from England in obeisance to her new Commanders command in order to meet this person and although the vessel 'Serenity' had plenty of people crossing its gangplank getting off from and on to that vessel this did not include the one whom she sought. Neither come to that had anyone in the neighbourhood noticed a man that bore the description of the one in the photograph that she carried with her. Thus she was left merely with the scenery, which as splendid as it might be hardly transported her into any holiday mood for she was conscious that perhaps after all she had failed on her very first assignment and now she dreaded the thought of having to confess her failure. She clicked her teeth in desperation as the visitors who had disembarked disappeared up the hill towards the town itself

Her mind turned back once again onto her father. Of course finding out that he too had been in the Service explained many things to her that had been a puzzle in the past. Things such as his long absences from home and her mother's reluctance to even speak about his employ. Perhaps it also explained why he had been so pedantic when it came to her own education at a time when she had no one but a sick mother with whom she could confide. Meanwhile she was now left to watch as a cargo boat plied its wares along the river in a dignified fashion and the gaunt Gothic type architecture watched its progress in a purposeful manner.

From the town a clock obediently chimed the hour at three and again at four o'clock by which time the daylight had already started to fade. The bevy of folk now returning to the cloisters of their craft made her realise that this visit was indeed proving futile. Still she supposed that reminiscing in the past would certainly not help to solve her present situation and almost against her will she routed in her pocket until her hands rested on her mobile. She realised of course that in her position it was frowned upon to ask for assistance, but what else was she now supposed to do, wait for the spring of the following year?

It was some time before she managed to get a response and even then her recipient was obviously none too pleased to be hearing from her at this time especially in what one could in one sense have regarded as her abject failure. But after a long silence during which she could only presume that her words were being carefully studied and possibly recorded, her response came, not that it appeared to be a willing impart from the receiver.

"Where are you now then?" She was sure that the voice responding was clicking in some frustration almost it appeared as if it had been a foregone conclusion that this novice was likely to fail with the mediocre task she had been allotted. By this time however Josie cared little for this person's tone.

"Why I'm sitting here enjoying some wonderful scenery with a full view of the river cosseting the craft sailing on it: Yet I probably consider that I might well have been better employed following the exploits of Kimberley Clark on television!"

"Need I remind you Miss Craven that you took an oath of allegiance to the Service and also promised not to question the orders you had been given?"

"At the time I never for one minute thought that your masters had sufficient funds to enable them to send me on a wild goose chase!"

"Hmm!" The other obviously swallowed back some of the rhetoric he was ready to expand upon. "So you actually let the suspect escape, am I right?"

"No, that is not right. In fact it is complete nonsense. I have never even spotted the person in question, at least not since my father's funeral. Well perhaps that is not completely correct, I thought that I caught a glimpse of the same man on the ferry as we crossed the Channel, but once we docked he miraculously managed to disappear!"

"By your comments I presume then that you flaunted yourself around until the person concerned became aware of your presence on that ship and consequently by the time you landed in Rotterdam he had already planned on how to make good his escape?"

"That is a complete load of cobblers too. I do happen to have my own code of ethics and advising the opposition that we are in the process of trailing them is not something that is included in this!" By this time a frustrated Josie had risen to her feet. For two pins she would have told the arrogant miscreant what he could do with his so-called job! What on earth did he think she was, some sort of idiot who would stand by and allow her father's killer to escape?

"Please hold your horses for a moment Miss Craven!" Perhaps by this time the speaker had prejudged what was going through her mind. "Have you a slip of paper handy? ----Good, I want you to write this number down, try to memorise it and then destroy it for it is the number of a contact in the area where you presently find yourself. I believe that he will be able to advise you on your next move, and when he informs you what you must do please do not let the Department down on that occasion Miss Craven!"

She cursed as the line went dead for in all truth she felt that she had not yet finished with this tiresome little mouthpiece. All she appeared to be left with was this number written down on the paper that she was supposed to memorise and then destroy. She supposed by that they presumed that she would eat it or something equally obnoxious. Even so she stared at the numbers trying her best to memorise them before then eventually destroying the paper.

Still even before she had the opportunity to try out this number for herself she saw yet another boat arrive and this time someone alighting who called out her name. Rather surprised she turned to see the stranger alighting from the Swiss 'Sapphire'. Yet this was not the one she was supposed to meet, she knew that from the photograph she had seen.

"Sorry, I'm afraid I sort of got held up. You are Miss Craven, Josie Craven whom I am speaking to?"

She nodded perhaps still at a loss to who this person was.

"Name is Frederick Hauser!" He obviously guessed her mood. "Sorry that Brad couldn't make it only he appears to have got himself a little tied up. Well quite a bit tied up really thanks to one Paul Butler!"

"Then-------!" A thousand and one thoughts crossed her mind.

"Oh I guess Brad will be all right. Let's say that he is a little incapacitated at the moment and therefore was unable to meet you for himself. The truth of the matter is however that Paul Butler appears to have skipped the country. He didn't know you were coming did he, by any chance?"

"I didn't send him an E Mail if that is what you are inferring, although in retrospect I am quite convinced I spotted the man leaving the same ferry that I was on!" Her voice she decided was unnecessarily cutting but then she excused herself. After all this was sheer frustration on her part.

"In that case it would appear that you have had a wasted journey!"

"I can't really agree with you on that point!" Now all she could think about was the valley where her father was supposed to have died. "I believe I need to go to this Loreley valley to see for myself the spot where----!"

She broke off conscious that her companion's eyes had opened wide at such a suggestion. "I accept that condolences are in order. It was hard lines about your father's demise. But don't you think you are now taking matters a little too far?"

"How the hell do you know about my father?" His words had surprised her. "Did you actually work with him or something?" She supposed one could say that her spleen had not yet settled down.

"I was in contact with your father prior to his death, yes Miss Craven. But perhaps the point of this argument is not so much a discourse on your late father but rather for us to seek out the present whereabouts of the one you term as being the perpetrator!"

"I have good enough reason to try to find the bastard. At the same time however I cannot claim that I am absolutely sure of your own motivation in this exercise!"

"I merely act as my country commands Miss Craven, something that I believe you also should endeavour to do and without question. But as you appear determined to visit the spot of your father's demise it is perhaps just as well that my car is parked here on the car park for it is, one might say, a little too far to walk from here!"

"But you came here by boat?"

"Yes, and my car is parked right here, for you see Frederick Hauser uses various means of transport to fulfil his obligations. So we will go –yes?"

It seemed only logical to follow him to where the Mercedes was parked even though she still felt a little reluctant to travel with this stranger who seemed to know everything there was to know about her. He noticed her expression and laughed.

"I had not thought to have seen someone in your position appearing to be so timid. I believe that you are an actress in your other life Miss Craven and I would have thought you would have already mastered the art of disguising raw emotions!"

Josie slammed the car door shut after she entered it, the sheer frustration now taking a firm hold on her. The other glanced at her rather puzzled for a moment before his face finally relaxed.

"I'm sorry. I suppose you have good reason to feel that way Miss Craven and therefore I beg for your indulgence on the subject!"

They fell into an agreed silence during the journey until they neared the Loreley Rock. It was a silence broken only as they passed one certain castle that dominated the vista from some height and for some reason Frederick felt inclined to comment upon it.

"The castle that you can see up there is apparently owned by a Mexican millionaire. I admit the place still appears to be as foreboding as ever but now in addition I believe that no one is allowed to get even close to it!" A tinge of perplexion appeared to touch the man's tone as he spoke but at the time Josie paid little attention for there was only one thing that now interested her.

Eventually he patiently drove the vehicle to the very top of the steep abyss. Spectacular views may have been in evidence from this vantage spot but such views were not for Josie as she clambered t her feet and Frederick obviously guessed her mood as he followed her to the very edge remaining close behind.

"Well you said that you wanted to see the place?" Her guide looked anxiously at Josie's expression as she came face to face with the point where her father had met his fate.

"I did!" She nodded her head adamantly ignoring the wind that was blowing her hair in quite a ridiculous fashion.

"And now that you have seen the place for yourself I think perhaps it is time for us to go!" Perhaps now he worried feeling that it was unsafe for her to be standing so close to the edge of the precipice especially in her state of mind. Believe me your father stood little chance of survival. It is a steep fall and in addition the rocks----!"

Josie turned away unwilling to hear any further details but Frederick had not finished. He handed her a small packet, fishing for it first in the knapsack he carried. "Your father's effects, such as they are. There are a couple of maps that he appeared to be carrying around, one of the river here and its immediate surrounds and one other which is not of this place. I do not understand the reason for his choice on that I am afraid!"

"My father was always very keen on his maps!" Josie took the packet deep in thought. As the man had said the first one was of the area as expected, but the other still folded neatly was a puzzle to her. Amongst the rest of the things in the packet there was a faded wallet and opening that brought a tear to her eyes for it contained a picture of herself and her mother when she had been just a child.

"Take them please if they are of any use to you. I believe you have already been given a number to contact?"

She nodded this man appeared to know everything, a state of mind that frightened her a little. "Then that is what you must do, but first I must take you away from this place and to somewhere where you will be able to spend the night. It is a guest house, not too far distance, but a place our people believe is quite safe. Strangely enough I did hear that the place was once a monastery, but of course it no longer functions as such. There you will be able to make your call and receive your new orders. I myself have to travel on to Ruddheim!"

"And these new orders I am supposed to have to received; how am I supposed to travel to any new venue? After all I did come here by coach!"

"Why not take the train? After all there is a good service along the Rhine and there is nothing left for you to do here now. But first you will naturally have to receive your new orders I believe Fraulein!"

Well she supposed it could be considered to be most unusual to be staying here in some old converted monastery but her hosts Maria and Hans went out of their way to make her feel welcome at the guesthouse, which she had to concede, was exceedingly well appointed.

Her first task however was to remember the contact number she had been given and once cloistered inside of her room she concentrated upon that task. Perhaps her confession that Paul Butler was not present in this location did little to please her respondent, that was however if the person at the other end of the line was not already aware that the eagle had already left the nest, for after a stark reminder of who exactly was employing her and consequently pulling her strings as if she was some puppet the crunch of the matter was to follow.

"For the sake of getting to the core of this discourse, we now believe that the person in question has possibly accepted a fee for services already tendered from his Al Queda employer. No doubt you are aware of the increased security threat to our own country in common with other European nations and we also have it on good authority that having concluded his business here in Northern Europe, Paul Butler is currently trying his hand in getting a passage on a cruise ship that will ultimately remove him from any fingers that happen to be pointing in his direction! Maybe you could consider that he possibly enjoys such scenery especially in the autumnal months of the year! Anyway we have already booked a passage for you on the Queen that is sailing to the Canaries and beyond, leaving its homeport tomorrow. Oh and by the way there is no necessity to adopt that expression!" Her caller must have now judged the immediate ponderings of her mind. "We have also managed to secure a cabin for you as well. Nothing too elaborate I must add, not with the current spending cuts taking effect, but I would suggest an inside cabin will suffice for your needs!"

Gee, thanks a million, by this time Josie's mind had focussed upon what she was supposed to wear for the occasion on formal nights as she hardly considered the gear she currently had with her to be suitable. There was another thing too, if she was in the Rhine valley and the ship sailed from Southampton on the following day, how was she supposed to get there?

"Just a minute perhaps you could tell me how I am supposed to get to this home port by tomorrow? I suppose you do mean Southampton?"

"No problem, the ship actually calls at Rotterdam on the following day. You see it has some additional passengers to pick up there, including yourself!"

"Let me get this right. You are suggesting that it is possible for Paul Butler to attempt to try his hand at some form of espionage on board the Queen, in fact on a British ship going anywhere for that matter?"

"Anything is possible Miss Craven. That is the reason why we wish you to present yourself on board if only to keep an eye on matters, as well as attempting to discover what exactly is running through Paul Butler's mind at this moment in time!"

"Excuse me if I am wrong but I came here under the distinct impression that I had been selected to claim some sort of justice after my father's death at the hands of this man, not to act as a nursemaid to him!"

"I believe you also swore allegiance to the Service Miss Craven. Therefore I am afraid that my advice to you now is to try to obey orders without question!"

Still pondering upon the dichotomies this phone call had opened in her mind Josie was trying to find some satisfaction in eating her evening meal when quite suddenly a dark satanic form swept into the place brushing aside anyone who happened to be standing in his way, with a presence that was obviously threatening. He spoke quickly in German which, even though Josie did not understand the language. She presumed was darkly demanding and she was in time to see the owners of that place, a hard working couple who slaved endlessly to make their business pay, almost quake in this man's presence before Hans made one bold attempt to shake his head in obvious denial at what was currently being levered out to him.

Instinctively she felt that the couple were trying their best to protect her even though Maria turned more than once with a frightened expression in her direction. Then the intruder obviously still in some doubt as to whether to believe their story followed the woman's eye and rested itself upon Josie. The latter witnessed the slight turning of the foot as it began to point now in her own direction and her worst fears were confirmed as she spotted that those feet were even then beginning to move across the room.

"Ah Fraulein Craven, you are enjoying our beautiful country no doubt?" She nodded gulping back the soup she had just placed inside of her mouth. "Your father I believe was the one who made such an untimely fall from the Loreley Rock. Am I correct in my assumption?"

She glanced up from the remains of her meal and instinctively disliked what she saw of this creature who could be described as one large bronzed skinned individual with his dark hair plastered back under some form of greasy layer and resembling more of a member of some unscrupulous Italian organisation than any Austrian and she immediately felt some understanding as to why the Austrian couple had exhibited a certain fear in the man's presence.

Perhaps now realising that the girl he faced had no intention of responding to him, the stranger obviously felt it right to introduce himself possibly hoping for some better response.

"The name is Marcos Aldermatt, Baron Aldermatt, and of course you must be the delightful Miss Craven whom I heard was visiting our village!" She had at first presumed that the thick set stranger had called in the Gausthaus for a drink and to now hear him mentioning her by name came a something of a shock to Josie. Indeed she must have appeared shaken for the big man crossed the floor to take her hand and she noticed the look of total recoil on both the face of the innkeeper and his wife. "It was such a terrible shock to hear about your father's accident my dear. I was resident in the castle at the time and therefore when I learnt that you were coming here I felt that I really needed to offer my condolences to you!"

"Actually I was just passing through the area and therefore it seemed to be quite natural for me to wish to see the spot where my father met his fateful accident!" Encouraged now by Maria she attempted to put a brave face on the situation. "Nevertheless I thank you for your concern Herr Aldermatt!"

"Baron Aldermatt. You see I have the good fortune to live at the castle, the one that you must have seen from the road. But I am forgetting myself, you must come and see my place for yourself!" Josie remembered Frederick pointing the place out to her. The sight of it had sent a cold chill down her spine at the time even though he had said that a Mexican millionaire had purchased the place privately. Well this person in front of her now may have been dark but to her eyes he certainly did not resemble any Mexican. "I will send Boris my chauffeur to collect you tomorrow and then maybe we will talk and you can tell me how this sorry state of affairs has effected you my dear!"

He smiled, an expression devoid of an emotion and it was simply a feature that served to highlight the cold feeling she had already felt upon first meeting the man. Yet if Josie was rendered speechless Maria was the one who was now not devoid from taking action for the woman's hands reached for the telephone. The result of her call arrived back at the Gausthaus almost before she could finish her evening meal and Frederick Hauser appeared looking almost as if he had a chip on his shoulder for being so disturbed.

"Well it appears totally unsafe to leave you alone for one single moment Miss craven without you striving to attract some unwanted attention!"

"I thought you said that you had urgent business to attend to in Ruddheim?" The stranger had vanished just as soon as Frederick had made his presence felt. Not that she felt sorry about that but at the same time this man doing his best to now annoy her was something she could have well done without.

"I had business to attend to yes, but this something I had to leave when I received Maria's call. You see as I have been charged to ensure that you have a stress free as possible transition, I doubt very much that my employers would offer me any kind of merit if anything should happen to you. From the look of things it also appears that you are well capable of attracting trouble if it happens to be around!"

"Well thank you very much for that vote of confidence!"

"I presume that by this time you will have already made your contact?" His eyes still flashed angrily for at the time Frederick Hauser was considering the other distraction he had in mind for that night!

"I have!" She closed her lips tightly on this account wondering at the same time why he should want to know. Anyway from what she had learnt an agent was not supposed to divulge matters of such privacy, however distasteful they might appear to be.

"And?"

"I do not believe I have any reason to tell you!"

"That you are going back to Amsterdam from whence you came?"

"Then you did know: You knew the outcome even before I contacted London?"

"Yes you see our mutual commander decided that by this time I had suffered enough at your hands. So much so that I do believe they are putting you on a boat. Even so for posterity's sake I would like to know just how stupid you have to act before the bosses decide to send you on a cruise?"

"In that case I needn't keep you any longer. I believe you mentioned catching a train? At that time I must have appeared to be stupidly naïve!"

"My own orders were to simply divorce myself from all other activities whilst you were here. Therefore in order that I might resume my own duties I intend to put you on that train, just in case you are tempted to get on the wrong one Miss Craven!" And with that off his chest Frederick Hauser pulled himself a chair up to the table where she sat and stubbornly sat facing her. "I suppose that you will have a room for me to spend the night here Maria?"

The woman nodded. To her mind the English certainly adopted some queer customs, but then she consoled herself that after all, the one who paid the bills was always in the right!

The journey had been tedious enough once Frederick had finally deposited her in that carriage on the train the following day that was apparently due to travel all the way back to the port. But perhaps the final irony of the situation was in having to catch that shuttle bus from one dilapidated old shed to a terminal building that appeared unaware of the onslaught that the berthing of the cruise ship would bring because the transport service appeared to be suffering from a knock on effect of the French strikes, all served to make Josie feel decidedly grumpy. Maybe the knowledge of what had already been made clear to her, such as the possibility of an Al Queda threat should have made her all the more eager to have obeyed her orders, but quite frankly this was not Josie Craven's style at all. Finally destroying the paper she had written the number on and wondering at the same time whether she should really have eaten it caused her to deem that this was not really what she was about, for after all her main if not only criteria for joining this Service in the first place had been to attempt to avenge her father's death. It had nothing at all to do with cavorting around some cruise ship in the mid Atlantic, but now it appeared she was forced to abide by this new set of rules, which had been haphazardly pitched in her direction.

Her thoughts turned again to the person she had known as Paul Butler for after she had seen him leave the ferry boat at this terminal with her own eyes he was now apparently somewhere else and quite some distance away from the scene. Not only that it had been suggested that the man had some sort of association with a world wide terrorist group. To her mind the whole idea seemed to be completely too far-fetched to even give it breath. And yet she was in no position to argue against her orders.

Attempting to check in at that International terminal was also to provide its own problems.

"Sorry Miss, but you do realise that there are only a bare six months left on your passport!" The ship's officer who challenged her glanced down at her apparently primitive luggage with a look of disdain. Perhaps he was joining her in wondering what on earth this woman was going to wear on formal nights! It was then fortuitously or otherwise that another standing in the background nodded his head in her direction. So it appeared that she had had been expected. Well, if the end could be said to justify the means the official let her pass but not before casting another piteous look in her direction. "Apparently there is a hire department on board ship Miss Craven, should you require to add to your wardrobe at any time!" It was the final slur before he allowed her to pass by and all she now prayed was that his voice had not been overheard by others who were round about at the time!

Gregg Anderson eyed his companion with a total look of disbelief and wondered whenever the man would chose to cease his seemingly never ending flow of rhetoric that issued from his lips at the same time as he toyed with those visual aids that appeared in the form of a large variety of maps, behaving to all the world that these indeed were sufficient to back up his present theory. After all he had come here in response to those stories relating to the supposed discovery off the site north of the Canary Islands and now all he was being bombarded with appeared to be a whole load of totally unrelated phenomena.

"To my mind at least it stands to sense!" The man appeared to be puffed up now and Gregg mused that perhaps he had at long last reached his final summing up of the one sided discourse that had taken many minutes to unravel. "In my opinion it must have been one massive volcanic eruption followed in its wake by the natural process of a tsunami that initially saw the advent of these Islands, spurred on to rise from the depth of the ocean bed to replace the lost city of Atlantis. After all such a phenomena is evident in Santorini, a place where others have in the past erroneously claimed that the lost city is buried. Now however these latest maps relating to the sea bed point us in the direction of quite a different scenario!" With this his companion pointed to one of the charts containing the same recent findings regarding some under sea construction that Gregg was already familiar with. "Of course we must concede that the Islands themselves retained some considerable volcanic activity for some considerable time after their emergence. In point of fact they did not all appear to have risen from the ocean bed at the same time and indeed a certain amount of volcanic activity can still be found in evidence in some of the younger Islands especially in the one I am particularly interested in. Thus these new creations must have provided a haven for the Barbary pirates during their fruitful activities. One could consider the number of people who disappeared from off the more Northern lands, I am thinking now of two places in particular although I guess there must have been others, besides one whole village of people who supposedly disappeared from Southern Ireland and also from a similar place in Iceland. Indeed the description of these people from the more Northern climes would well fit the description often apportioned to the gaunches or early inhabitants of the Islands. As the main focus of such kidnapping activities was to sell white slaves on the markets of Africa, the Islands would have provided extremely good staging posts for these pirates to have initially held such slaves. Yet not all of these people did finish up in the bazaars, whether this was because they managed to escape into the hinterland or rebelled or the market trade eventually dried is another question!"

"Well I guess it's a pretty enough story bit not one I suggest that provides the reason for me travelling here to this meeting with you. You now claim that you have maps relating to the positioning of this lost city that disappeared during some tidal wave, but I feel I need to remind you that we are marine biologists and not deep sea divers, even if it was possible for such divers to exist at the depths you suggest!"

"You are right of course at least in ninety nine percent of cases, but on the other hand there still happens to be one place where volcanic eruptions have been the forerunner to chasms forming underneath the land itself where the ocean is currently eating it away. Such a place could have its uses for gathering samples!"

"Samples of what and for what? Although I have always had the greatest respect for your brain quotient Helmut, this madcap philosophy now makes me wonder about the quota of common sense that was allotted to you!"

"Sense?" The other man shrugged. "But surely it is our forte to collect samples of marine life as well as other manifestations based on a regular depth, more especially if one is also being paid for undertaking such a task. One could say that in such endeavours we might even be adding something of scientific interest to our generation. After all I was given to understand that as marine biologists that was what we were about! Besides I also mentioned that such efforts on our part are to be rewarded by a rather handsome payout!"

"What exactly do you mean by that?"

"A mere fifty thousand U.S. dollars with all expenses paid. How does that suit you?"

"It strikes me to question exactly who is the paymaster. You see I prefer to know who I am supposed to be working for!"

"It is quite legitimate if that is what you are inferring. In actual fact it is for an Englishman, someone with something to do with national defence. You know the type and it is not appropriate to question why the British Government should want such information!"

"I believe you also said, all expenses. For starters how do you propose that we get to this place and what about the necessary equipment we will need?"

"Such incidentals will all be provided for. Did I mention that we are actually due to depart from our present surrounds on a British cruise ship?"

"No, you didn't! But having done so you now convince me that the whole idea is quite ridiculous. For starters cruise ships pause only briefly at recognised ports!"

"The ship will take us where we want to go and it will afford us the time to complete our task. Not only that but it will also provide us with a degree of anonymity, an aspect that our employers demand from us. In addition the ship will also take us to other places that the British Government now appear to have an interest in!"

"And these other places are then?"

"An archipelago of islands lying some distance further south to the Canaries where our paymasters require us to carry out some preliminary investigations. In such a case I believe that ours is certainly not to question their reasoning for after all, all that we are required to do is to enjoy a cruise, pocket fifty thousand U.S. dollars and carry out the sort of survey we have been trained to do. Surely you cannot find anything to argue in that!"

Gregg shrugged his shoulders. It appeared that his companion was only too eager to undertake such a mission and after all he supposed they were friends as well as colleagues. Therefore he could see no reason why he did not trust Helmut's motivation in all this. "So when are we expected to leave on this expedition?"

"The day after tomorrow, from Rotterdam in actual fact! Apparently the ship is calling in there to take on board more passengers. We ourselves have been considered to be part of that number. So now having expounded myself, what do you have to say?"

"What can I say? You appear to have the mission well organised. In fact I really don't know why you didn't take off without me. Myself? Well I would have much preferred to have had a little more notice and a little more detail as to what our employers are about. But then I suppose that if you are satisfied then I must be prepared to accept your arrangements!"

"Good man! I promise that I will fill you in with a few more details when we get underway!"

"As you say although I must confess with this on the cards I thought something would have been said at a recent meeting I attended before I left England

His companion frowned. "It is always possible I suppose that only a few know about our current briefing. There is something else however that I have not yet mentioned. Apparently there is currently a female whom we have been requested to avoid at all costs as she could prove to be detrimental to our cause. Actually I believe she is a familiar face on children's television!" Gregg's jaw must have sagged just a little for his companion's face changed. "I believe you are already aware if such a situation?" The voice was now terse.

"I believe that I have already met the person in question. As a matter of fact we were travelling companions when I crossed the Channel but then she left Rotterdam to catch a coach to go to the Rhine or somewhere. Therefore I doubt whether she will prove to be any problem!"

"Upon that matter we shall see. Just remember this though, we cannot afford to take any chances!"

"In that case what exactly are we supposed to do if we run into her again?"

"That will of course depend upon the circumstances!"

His companion's lips were obviously closed now upon the matter and therefore Gregg conceded that he might just as well push the matter to the back of his mind. After all, seeing Josie Craven again after she herself had set out to meet someone on the Rhine was an extremely unlikely event and could be discarded as such. Strange really but he didn't really feel that he wanted to discard the memory of Josie Craven for the girl had fascinated him in more senses than one!

★ ★ ★ ★

Chapter Three

In retrospect she supposed that the boat could be considered to be pretty full, consequently her first challenge she supposed was the life boat drill, when equipped with her life jacket she was to find herself hustled into a packed restaurant still full of people eating their breakfast. The result of this entrance however meant that the restaurant emptied pretty quickly, folk now pushing aside the food that they were in the process of eating to return to their cabins for their own life jackets, all of which was not really a pretty sight!

Still the gradual motion of the craft coupled as it was with the lapping of the waves against its side provided a cacophony of sound that could easily have lulled one to sleep whilst the Jacuzzi bubbled invitingly but to which no one had yet ventured perhaps because the waters of the swimming pool, which lay adjacent to them appeared to be a little more turbulent as it shed over onto the surrounding deck. Even so there were those who were doggedly determined to circumnavigate the ship in order to complete the obligatory mile walk that they had set for themselves under a sky that was intermittently flanked with dark clouds, which for a time appeared rather ominous

Sat there on deck as the reaches of the English Channel and the Celtic Sea passed out of view and watching as the other chattering passengers passed backwards and forwards along close by to her Josie decided not for the first time that the whole of this scenario could be termed as being ridiculous. The very notion that she had actually managed to pass through security wearing that weapon for starters was completely ludicrous, although she did remember that after checking her passport she had been motioned through a side door away from the rest of the travellers so she supposed her masters could be called to account on her making the decks of this ship. But then she realised that it was not the first time she had earned herself an easy passage, for no one had scanned her when she had initially left from Hull. Nobody, but nobody could be so lax, unless they had been pre-warned of her coming.

Now however this posing on the deck was an irritation to her for in truth since they had left Rotterdam she had searched practically every last inch for signs of the man she now sought, every salon, every bar, each restaurant had all undergone her eagle eye but of this character there had been no sign whatsoever. So after reaching the conclusion that he must be skulking somewhere in his cabin to secrete him from public view, she had vied this space where she hazarded a guess that everyone on that boat would pass at least on one occasion. Her eyes suddenly prickled in anticipation, for just behind the bar waiter who was presently plying his trade about that part of the deck she caught sight of another figure. But this, unless she was very much mistaken was not Paul Butler and without thinking she grabbed hold of her magazine and held it up to her face, behaving for all the world as if the sun had just caught her eyes. For this person who no longer appeared to be on his own was one person she felt that she would rather not see at this present moment. In fact her determination to remain anonymous overshadowed her inbuilt curiosity as to what Gregg Anderson was doing on this craft. From behind her paper she eyed his companion and wondered whether this was the contact he had planned on meeting in Amsterdam. Not that it was any of her business of course for Gregg Anderson was after all a free person, but the fact that he happened to be here in the same situation as herself did little to quieten her spleen. Not that at the time she need to have worried for the man, appearing to be immersed in his own thoughts passed her by without a second thought and all she was left with was an insatiable sense of curiosity as to what he was doing here.

He had passed from out of her line of vision when she received the invitation, delivered by a smartly dressed cabin -boy, who hung around after handing it to her for an obvious tip. Wondering how this youth had managed to find her she hardly hesitated before breaking open the seal. Inside there was an invitation with her name embedded in gold leaf to attend the captain's cocktail party that very same evening, whilst the youth hopped from one leg to the other obviously waiting for a response.

Immediately her mind floated onto her dinner wear, which was at the time strictly inadequate. She knew of course that one could hire the necessary from on board but she had also realised that there were a selection of boutiques on board and such a shopping expedition would no doubt help to while away the hours. Not that she felt that she could afford some of the prices they were asking for this was no market trader. But for once she decided that she would have to dig deep into her resources, a matter that chided her but which was obviously strictly necessary and having made the decision, gave the boy her affirmative response.

Thus most of the remainder of that day was to be spent agonising over the gear she should wear for the occasion. Fortunately one of the women who frequented the boutique took pity on her and consequently Josie was to emerge looking less like someone from St Trinian's and more in keeping with what was required on board.

"You will still have to do something with your hair of course!" The woman she supposed was still only trying to be helpful and Josie running her fingers through her tousled mop wondered what weird and wonderful things could be applied to at least make it lie flat. "You are new to all of this aren't you?" Now the woman appeared to be sympathetic as Josie nodded in response. "Look don't worry, I will have a word with Jean the hairdresser on board and see what she can suggest, that is providing that you allow me to do this for you?"

Not knowing what else she could do in the circumstances Josie agreed and without further ado the woman made to leave her kiosk and move to one just across the shopping mall. The fact that the two women were obviously talking about her and weighing her up had long since ceased to worry Josie. "She can take a look at you now!" Her confidante from the boutique eventually returned triumphant. "Don't worry about the clothes you have purchased, I will hold onto them for you until she has finished with you!"

She later supposed the transformation in anyone terms was quite surprising, for with little ado Josie was shortly to find her long locks shorn and her head complimented with a fashionable bob cut. "It ought to be easy for you to care for yourself as well!" The hairdresser appeared triumphant at the change she had wreaked and glancing in the mirror Josie was surprised to see those large eyes looking back at her and possibly chiding her for her positive neglect in previous times. "I will arrange for you to go to the make up department!" The hairdresser still frowned when she viewed the blotches she considered to spoil her coiffure. Therefore the whole matter had apparently been taken out of her hands and Josie began to possibly realise why such invitations were required to go out in the morning to allow their recipients time to prepare. Still land was obviously nowhere in sight and neither did she have any quarry to bait so Josie supposed that it was as good a way as any to spend the time as well as the money currently in her pocket. But after all this was once in a lifetime and tonight she vowed to forget all about Paul Butler and Gregg Anderson as a matter of fact and concentrate her attention on the debonair captain of the ship.

Debonair and handsome were only two of the adjectives she could have used to describe that Captain who lingered over her hand a little longer than one would have expected that night. Obviously of Mediterranean descent the man had kept his exaggerated good looks well into his middle age and years of experience had taught him how to use these to their full effect.

"Positively charming!" His long eyelashes fluttered as he finally released her hand after holding onto it far longer than what was deemed to be necessary. "And I understand quite famous as well!" So that was the reason why she had been invited. This one must also be a television addict.

"I would hardly term myself as being that Sir!" Her response was ready on her lips to emit once that question had been expounded.

"Ah but then it is seldom such perfectionists like yourself do allow themselves to be classed as famous. But on the other hand you appear to be causing a bit of a stir right here on my boat so it is obvious to all that you must have a following. Not that I would blame anyone now that has had the good fortune to meet you, not withstanding those who have previously met you and already regard you highly!"

Josie bristled at his words for to her mind they seemed to reiterate that other meeting when the spectre of Baron Aldermatt had crossed her path. Thus she glanced around for some means of escape. Her current thoughts she accepted were ridiculous and yet his introduction was taking far too long and there were others all waiting their turn to meet the Captain of this ship and eyeing her as if she was something of an intruder for monopolising the great man's time. Still perhaps the man himself eventually realised his own personal charge of the evening. "Please forgive me my dear for monopolising so much of your time but I confess your description matches perfectly the one that was given to me by an old acquaintance of mine whom you apparently met recently. Forgive me if I am incorrect but you were in the Rhine region recently weren't you?" Josie gulped something in response but perhaps by this time the Captain had realised that others were currently waiting to be introduced. "Do help yourself to a drink and join the others my dear!" He motioned to where a group of people had already gathered and switching her eyes across onto them Josie was bewitched as they came to rest on the form of Gregg Anderson.

Which of them was surprised the most by this meeting it was initially difficult to say although from Gregg's point of view he had now to take in the new image of this girl and could only relate that he found it to be very fetching indeed. Of course the man would choose that moment to cross over to her side and ask her to dance, almost indeed as if he was in the process of denying the tumulus thoughts that were currently besetting her mind, thoughts that were indeed settling upon this man's presence here. Yet on the contrary Gregg appeared completely debonair and at ease in that tuxedo almost indeed as if he was used to being dressed in such apparel and dashing any such thoughts she had about him into insignificance with a look that most girls would probably have died for. Listening to the orchestra as they waited for the remaining guests to be introduced to the Captain she supposed had provided a pleasant interlude which had helped to soothe a few of the furrows that were in danger of gathering, but to dance with Gregg at this time was possibly the last thing she really wanted

To refuse however she supposed would have led to even more raised eyebrows and probably more questions and therefore perhaps this was the main reason why she allowed him to guide her onto the dance floor. Yet once there she was to find herself almost moulded into his arms as their bodies began to intertwine to the lilt of a foxtrot. Indeed if Josie closed her eyes she could now almost forget who her partner was. But then of course Gregg, naturally enough had to go and spoil things.

"You appear to have impressed our Captain back there. In fact I could almost sense the queue behind you becoming restless!"

Josie felt her limbs stiffen. She realised that he had been watching all the time she had been in the Captain's company but there was no way she was now going to confess her own thoughts on that particular encounter.

"I think you are mistaken. The Captain for his part was merely attempting to be his charming self!"

"And to you more than anyone else. Not that I particularly blame the man although I wouldn't have guessed he was a television addict!"

"Can we leave it there please!" Perhaps her fortune was about to change for just then she spotted Helmut entering the lounge. "I believe your friend appears to be looking for you!"

He glanced over her shoulder and then shrugged. "Maybe Helmut can be left to look after himself for a while!" His look into her face appeared to be almost penetrating, whilst his own face drew closer to her own so that she began to feel enveloped in some magical spell

"I thought that you said you had to meet up with you colleague in Amsterdam?" Desperately she allowed her own question to preclude any he had to ask of his own.

"I did, I have brought him here with me!" He motioned in Helmut's direction who was currently still sitting at one of the tables in the lounge. "But then you yourself gave me to understand that you had to travel along the Rhine to meet up with a colleague?"

"That I did only to find that the person concerned had already left. As it was a wasted journey I sought to console myself with a little over indulgence in the form of this cruise!"

" No doubt your over indulgence did not stop there. But having said that I must admit that the new hairstyle suits you. I always considered Kimberley Clark's to be rather severe, a factor that helped to conceal at the time the fact that underneath all those dressing's lay a damned attractive woman!" She blushed almost against her will. She certainly did not want to get tied up with this man not at this stage. "And now you have managed the feminine way of acknowledging a compliment as well. A factor I find most surprising. But we are standing in the way of the other guests at this spot. You spoke of my companion, well why not come and meet him for yourself again!"

She wondered at a later stage whether she did have any alternative rather than blindly allow him to leave her.

"Helmut, guess who I have just spotted? The female I met on the boat crossing from Hull remember?"

The Dutchman made to shake her hand in a most professional manner and yet at the same time Josie was under the distinct impression that the man was not overjoyed to see her. Maybe this was because the Dutchman was at the time engrossed in his own thoughts and resented such an intrusion. Still little more could be said for the formalities were now over, the photographs had all been posed for, the music stopped and the Captain made his few words of address before they all retired to the dining room. Any previous concepts she might have been holding that these invited guests were destined to sit at the Captain's table that night were soon proved to be wrong. For in truth apart from sampling a little of the taster dish the Captain begged to be excused owing to the pressure of work and his presence on the bridge being required. Besides upon reflection she deemed she should have noticed that there were far too many people who had been introduced to the Captain that evening to be able to sit down at any one table not withstanding the fact that the Captain, if he so spied an opportunity much preferred to serve himself in the Bistro rather than pander to the formalities that the English appeared to expect. Consequently they were to find their name places already allocated to tables of various sizes and Josie herself found that she was destined to share a table with Gregg and his companion.

Much to her surprise however it was the Dutchman who appeared to want to initiate the conversation, for initially she had been determined that the other had not been quite as pleased as his friend to see her there. "So tell me Miss Craven how a woman destined to travel to the Rhine valley should find herself present at this function here tonight. I presume you boarded at Rotterdam as we did ourselves although I must confess that I do not remember seeing you waiting to board in the Terminal buildings there?" His eyes when he asked the question in perfect English without any shadow of an accent appeared to be deep and penetrating. Still conversation of any kind now appeared preferable to sitting there in stony silence like the other woman seemed to now desire.

"As I already stated, my plans were changed at the last moment. The person I was supposed to contact at Koblenz was no longer there for some reason and I was therefore advised to partake of this cruise adventure. But tell me Helmut, what is it in this voyage that should prove to be of such interest to a couple of Marine biologists?"

He obviously abhorred the fact that his own questions had been turned about and looked towards a person who appeared to be travelling on her own with splendid anticipation. "Would you care to dance madam whilst we are waiting for our next course?" Perhaps for the first time that evening the woman concerned now appeared to brighten up and showed little hesitation in taking up Helmut's offer which resulted in Gregg and Josie being left at the table on their own.

"I suppose that one could consider the idea to be novel, dancing between courses I mean. In which case may I request your hand again between the main course and the sweet?"

He put the question in such a manner that Josie felt bound to laugh although laughter had not been on her initial agenda for that evening. "By the way that style highlights your features. You want to wear your hair like that even after tonight!" To Josie's mind however it was not so much a question of her appearance that lay uppermost in her head but rather the fact that the man had obviously avoided answering her initial question as to why two marine biologists were into cruising on the decks of that boat when she felt equally sure that the two of them would possibly have felt more at home in the waters that lapped its port and starboard!

The silence that followed his remark was everything if not deafening, still she later had to admit that she had not expected him to ask her to dance right there and then and thus she must have appeared something of a gawky schoolgirl when he eventually posed that question. In one sense she supposed it was inevitable for their conversation appeared to have completely dried up whilst at the same time the other two from that table were already on the floor as were many of the others who were present that evening, even if to her mind the melody must now have almost finished. Yet she took his hand without question for now in her own mind this appeared to be a way out from the uncomfortable stance of being left there on their own and she noted Helmet's eyes looking almost clinically in their direction as he twirled close by with his partner.

What she had never expected however was the feeling of being in this man's arms even if the duration was cut to an absolute minimum due to the orchestra feeling it was high time they took a break from their labours and anyway the tables now cleared, the chefs were already conducting their own dance of frenzy in an effort to see their next course served whilst it was still fit to be eaten. The Captain returned briefly during this course to circulate around the tables and wish all well before he claimed that duties on the bridge still demanded his attention and then quite suddenly it was Gregg's turn to remind her that they hadn't really finished their dance and anyway she had promised to allow him to take her onto the floor between the main course and the sweet!

Once again she sensed Helmut's eyes upon her as she rose from the table and the discomfort she experienced made her turn to Gregg in an effort to glean some explanation of this man's attitude. "Somehow I don't think that your friend approves of me being here!" She tried her best to keep her tone nonchalant.

"Oh Helmut, don't take any notice of him. After all he is a Dutchman and probably unfamiliar with our ways. Having said that however the man is extremely good at his profession and is a highly qualified marine biologist!"

"So does that mean you intend to start fishing off the back of the boat then?" At least her nonchalant attitude brought a smile to his lips.

"Most definitely not I can assure you, therefore there is no earthly need why you should want to disown me. But we do intend to undertake some diving off one of the Canary Islands in order to collect some samples for posterity. So until we get to that place I am more than content to enjoy the company of one beautiful female, even if she does pose more of a mystery to me than anything else. Therefore if I solemnly promise not to pressurise you for your side of the story that must be lurking close by, will you promise me to look favourably upon my presence during the next few days?"

She smiled for there seemed to be little else she could do under the circumstances and after all Gregg Anderson did not make an entirely bad companion on that sea voyage. Indeed as he swept her away in time to the music she appeared to have more and more difficulty in remembering what she was doing there in the first place!

They made their first designated stop on the Island of Maderia some two days later. Still without catching a glimpse of Paul Butler Josie had confined herself to toying through the mass of shore excursions that were on offer at that place before finally deciding that behaving like some lost tourist was just not on. She had been sent here to do a job, she owed it to her father's memory to complete this task and that did not include gallivanting about on any shore excursions. She would have had some excuse if she had spotted the suspect and was in the act of following him but she had failed dismally to do this and yet she had been assured that he was sailing on this same craft.

Pouting a little as she sat on deck pondering on her next move she spotted Gregg returning from his session up in the gym, or rather it was Greg who first spotted her; not of course that she was attempting to hide herself away at the time. Since that first night at the Captain's reception, the two of them had appeared to get on famously together, although she could hardly say the same about his colleague, the Dutchman. Indeed Helmut appeared to have been super critical of her, reminding her of some irritated father who was vetting the associations of his offspring. That thought alone was enough to make her laugh although she based this apparent jealous streak more on his nationality than anything else, for what was regarded as favourable mannerisms in one country was often not thought of in the same light somewhere else.

"So now what do you think you are doing----- appealing for inspiration?" He had paused by her chair and Josie caught the odour emitted from his body. Almost in desperation she picked up the leaflet of shore cruises. "Oh so you are pondering on those. Personally I believe riding up in that cable car to come down the mountain side in a wicker basket might be more your style!"

She allowed the flow of disdain to show in her eyes at such a suggestion. Quite frankly of all the tours on offer afternoon tea at Reid's seemed to be more in her style. Plus there was an additional opportunity for her to sort of crowd search from that place, far more at any rate than in cruising down any hillside in a wicker basket. "I'm quite surprised you've been to the gym this morning. I thought you would have got all the exercise you needed from your underwater exploits!"

"No underwater exploits today I am afraid. This is Madeira remember!"

"So what difference does that make for it is usually linked with the Canaries on such cruises?"

"For one thing the water is far too deep for us to carry out the sort of survey we have in mind!"

"And it won't be deep when we get to the Canaries?"

"Not quite so deep especially in certain places. Remember they are situated far closer to the continent than this place is!"

"Then you are free?"

"I was until a few minutes ago and then I realised that you were waiting for me to take you somewhere!"

"That is not fair, I was merely sat here contemplating. Anyway surely you have your friend to consider and what he wants to do whilst we are here!"

"You mean Helmut? The man my dear is a positive loner. Oh we work together when we have a task to complete but socially I prefer to find my own company and I believe that I have just found her!" He smiled almost winsomely in her direction and Josie felt her determination beginning to waiver a little. "So if you don't fancy a ride in a wicker basket have you decided what you would like to do instead?"

"How do you fancy a little afternoon tea at Reid's?" At least she managed to pose the question.

"You want to go for afternoon tea at Reid's, but surely that is more in keeping for the older generation?"

"It also promises relaxation and a chance to shop window the Island, which if we are only here for the day is possibly the best thing for us to do!"

"O.K. then have it your own way. Not that it would have been my own first choice but then I am glad to bend to your superior wisdom in such matters!"

"Well it will give you an opportunity to talk and you can tell me about your work. After all I really can't get to know much about it at all with Helmut persisting with his deviations!"

"And what is more you don't think Helmut will be turned on with the idea of afternoon tea at Reid's? Well, that is a fair enough comment Miss Craven, in which case shall we deposit our names at the tour reps office?"

Madeira at this time of the year dispelled the notion that the constant rain brought to the home country. It was exceedingly pleasant and served to lift the spirits from out of the doldrums thus Josie mused as she sat later that afternoon taking tea with Gregg and feeling thankful that she had not spent her leave merely tramping the streets of Funchal. With the sun currently casting a halo effect on the land surrounding them it was easy to begin to forget her true motivation for coming here and the man she had yet to find. Oh yes, she admitted that she had kept one eye open for his likeness on the way here but had finally given up that quest as something of a lost cause. Besides she had a charming escort to entertain her and deliberately pinched herself on one or two occasions less she should find that he was captivating her with some sort of spell he had cast over her. For Gregg's part, he was intrigued with this female that others had tried to warn him about for he was by this time quite convinced that they had been mistaken in their diagnosis.

Matters may have continued in adopting the old colonial mannerisms with the tea and scones provided in a glass sort of shelter from the penetrating rays of the afternoon sun, except that something was to happen that resulted in Josie being wrested from this land of make belief into reality, and the cause of this was the sight of Helmut Schmitz, not this time on his own but speaking rather urgently with another party. And it was the second person that Josie instantly recognised, for surely the girl needed no photographs to compare the likeness of her father's killer.

"Hey, what's the matter? Is there something wrong?" Her companion was obviously startled at her sudden movement but then Josie had seen the pair walking along the main road together on the outside of the establishment from her hillside position.

Without thinking Josie's hand had strayed to the place where she had previously secreted that weapon on her person. After all she had already been given her orders. And then she remembered that the weapon was no longer there, for hadn't she herself removed it in the heat of the day when she wished to wear her shorts and placed it in the safety deposit box back in her cabin? The thought of her action caused a definite moan to escape from her lips, and now believing that the girl must be ailing in some way, Gregg Anderson jumped to his feet.

"Why I do believe that is Helmut passing us by on the road outside!" His eyes had followed her own but there was an inscrutable expression upon the man's face as he spoke. "Now what on earth is he doing here, he told me that he planned to stay on the boat because the place was of no particular interest to him and I presumed that was because the terrain here was not suitable for diving purposes for the man only exists to fulfil one purpose I am afraid!"

"He appears to have found himself a friend anyway!" The two were now passing from out of her line of vision much to her frustration yet there was still little she could do about it.

"That appeared to be a certain Paul Butler of all people. I knew the man when he was still a boy in sixth form before he aspired to go off to one of those fancy Universities. I don't know where Helmut knows him from, but there again the Dutchman may be a valued colleague of mine but he can be something of a mystery in many ways. Still I wonder how he managed to get here, I'm certain that he didn't travel with us on the boat!"

At least her companion did appear to be as much in the dark over that matter as what she was herself yet it seemed as if a certain cloud had been cast across the afternoon's proceedings and she doubted whether she would be able to settle back down again. Fortunately the rest of the party now appeared ready to make a move so that problem did not apply. Again she looked for the pair once they were outside of those walls around the garden but naturally enough there was now no sign.

"Tell me something, why did the sight of them together unnerve you so much?" So her companion had noticed her agitated state she decided as he linked arms with her and for a time words to respond to his question tended to escape her until she remembered something that Gregg had said previously.

"Because of what you said previously concerning Helmut and his refusal to get off the boat if he couldn't perfect his diving skills!"

"But of course!" She knew that he didn't believe her words and yet he appeared prepared to leave the matter at that, remarking instead on the various sights as they wended their way back again to the boat.

Once on board she left him for she determined to watch at a discrete distance for the sight of the others returning, and again he did not appear to want to argue with her but instead stipulated that he had already booked another session on the training machines for that afternoon. Thus once she was left on her own for once Josie did not know whether to feel glad or sorry and she steeled herself determinedly by putting her new career to the forefront of her mind.

Her determination was not destined to last for long however. Sitting sharing a table with Gregg and Helmut for the meal that evening she soon became aware that the Dutchman's eyes were fastened upon her as if in some unfathomable way the man was trying to sort her out. It was therefore left to Gregg to attempt to make an attempt at polite conversation possibly because the man himself was beginning to feel embarrassed at the situation and the feeling of impasse that hung around their table. In a way Josie swore silently to herself because it was not through choice she was sharing a table with these two, but after the seating on the Captain's reception evening it seemed to be expected that the three would prefer it to be that way and in any case the dining staff obviously took a dim view to anyone claiming that they wanted to dine on their own, for this was not how the tables were arranged. Besides with Gregg, Josie now felt that she did share some common ground, although this was certainly not true as far as his companion was concerned.

Perhaps it was Gregg himself who cut something of the terse atmosphere alluding between the other two that one could have cut providing they had a sharp enough knife and in his own way he determined to put the matter to rights.

"We never expected to see you away from the boat after what you said previously Helmut, and yet we spotted you climbing the hill whilst we were enjoying the view from the gardens at Reid's this afternoon. At the time I believe that you also had someone with you?"

"Of course you are speaking now of Paul Butler I presume. Actually he had some interesting information to relate to me!"

"The first thing I would like to ask is how did he get there? I am sure that he is not on the boat!"

"He isn't, but then in case you have not heard of them there are certain objects that fly in the sky that we call aeroplanes, and which often incidentally provide a faster means of travel!" Helmut looked disdainful. Almost indeed as if he now wished that he were flying as well to relieve the tedium of this boat that moseyed along at a steady pace.

"So did he want to see you about something special?" Josie was surprised that Gregg had mouthed the question for her.

"He did. Apparently he believes that our mutual friend who is presently sharing a table with us wishes to kill him!" Both pairs of eyes now focussed themselves on her and there was no way that Josie could hide her embarrassment.

"But why on earth should he want to think that? He doesn't even know the girl?" Again Gregg had ignored her gasp and was wading into the matter as if she was a piece of useless flotsam sitting on the sidelines.

"Because apparently he says that she believes that he killed her father. A rather rash statement I agree but one which he was pedantic about!"

"No, don't go Josie, let's hear your side of the story on this saga!" He had caught her hand as she made to rise.

"I believe that to be the truth yes although what it matters outside of the two concerned I cannot imagine!"

Gregg whistled as a thought occurred to him. "So that was your true reason for going up the Rhine valley on that coach was it? You expected to find the man there?"

"I had it on good authority that he was, yes but obviously I was mistaken. Then at a later stage I was tipped off that he was possibly on this boat but it appears that I was mistaken about that as well!"

"Look who exactly are you working for Josie. This is hardly a script for children's television!"

"I prefer to keep that matter to myself!"

"According to what Paul said she happens to be working for British Intelligence!"

"Is he right Josie?" Perhaps a sudden anxiety had crept into Gregg's voice by this time and Josie could not help but wonder why. Had he in all truth something that he wished to hide as well?

"I am not prepared to answer that question, but apparently my father was working for them and he was killed because of it!" Her jaw line was set in a firm expression as she decided that she had heard quite enough and therefore had no wish to stay around for any inquisition whatever damned right they claimed that they had. "And now please excuse me. That way you can get on with your little digressions out of earshot from me. Also in actual fact I believe that there are more pressing matters on my time than to sit here fending and proving!" Her hands were shaking as she rose from that table, all she hoped was that her jelly type legs would support her long enough to leave the restaurant. In a way she wondered why Gregg did not attempt to stop her this time around but then felt glad that he hadn't for surely the air would prove to be much fresher on the outside.

Thus the two she had left behind had cause to explain to the headwaiter where madam had disappeared to and the one of Philippine descent questioned as if this was indeed an insult to their cooking.

"Madam doesn't feel too well, too much sun I think!" At least Gregg made an attempt to formulate a reasonable excuse for her.

"But madam will miss her meal. This will not do at all!" Resolute the man in charge of the dining procedure clicked his fingers and immediately several of the other waiters emerged from some hidey-hole. "Please arrange for madam to have her meal in her cabin. I believe the lady is not feeling too well at the moment although I did not consider the sun had been all that strong today!" It was then that Gregg smothered a smile for he could almost imagine Josie being followed to her cabin with this bevy of restaurant staff and he supposed this thought helped to relieve some of the tension that had suddenly beset him as he began to see Josie Craven in quite a new light!

Chapter Four

The water lapping over the sides of the swimming pool like the waves of a tide lapping onto the foreshore and making a cacophony of sound that was gentle to the ears was the only indication of the movement of the craft as it moved along the coastline of Tenerife heading towards its designated pause in La Gomera. Yet the sun, playing on the upper deck of the boat served to relieve all possible tensions of the spirit. As it was still early on in the day the walkers who normally broke the continuity of the scene with their determination to cover the required distance each day in miles had not yet surfaced and consequently it proved an ideal place for contemplation upon what the ancients must have thought when they had first spotted that Island as a black towering mass rising up from the ocean floor and was given to wonder whether they viewed this as a spectre of evil or a point of refuge when they had dared to venture forth to take a closer look from the ocean's massive expanse. Perhaps it was no small wonder that these people who had first viewed this cluster of

Islands at the gateway to the Atlantic, as being the site of that once ill fated land and above all the sentinel of Teide stood firm in its role as guardian of the place.

It now seemed fitting indeed that the namesake of the Queen of one ancient Icenic tribe should now indeed ply the same waters that served as the playground of basking whales and dolphins that today were visited frequently by the tourist trade. Yet at this early hour that trade had not yet frequented these waters and therefore such marine life was to be left in peace.

Josie watched for even now, as the ship ploughed its way through the remaining nautical miles Helmut was already beginning to show a marked enthusiasm for he had joined her out on the deck and appeared to be as excited as a schoolboy as he wondered whether such dreams as he had already metered out would finally come to fruition.

Still it was strange to notice when they finally pulled into port two the passengers disembarking with their luggage. But then she was not to know that their cabin had already been allocated to another for a restless night spent tossing and remembering what she considered to be her own personal misfortune, determined Josie to escape from the vicinity of La Gomera where the boat was to dock the following day. For one thing she knew that the divers had planned on being active at that place. Indeed that had been obvious from the time Helmut had spotted the advert for shore and boat diving and whilst the Island itself was quite small in relation to the length of others, it's capital had little to amuse oneself for an extended period and the excursions out did not particularly inspire her. Besides there was always a chance that in such a small place she would run into Gregg and his friend, and this after the previous day she did not want. Therefore having carefully considered her options Josie decided to catch the regular ferry boat across to Los Christianos where there was at least an abundance of life and consequently a place where she could lose herself for a few hours. Still there was one other thing to consider and that was one of the airports to Tenerife was situated close by and consequently not knowing what chance might possibly throw in her path she carefully donned the weapon beneath her clothing and was thankful that there was no internal security checks between these two Islands. Perhaps she had good reason to feel glad about her decision when she was waiting for the ferry boat to appear around the harbour wall she spotted the two of them negotiating the tunnel to approach the Playa de Cueta for now it appeared that Helmut's main objective was to gain access to the rocky piers leading out into the sea and ideal for what the man had in mind. The place itself was quiet only recently developed with a tree lined promenade and a small beach of shingle and black sand. Yet from its shore it extended a view of Teide partially masked halfway from its summit with swirling cloud. But it was still the appeal of Tenerife and the frequent ferry service across those straits that appealed far more to Josie.

"Probably see you in the Plaza de las Americas when you get back!" For his part Gregg had appeared non too pleased at her suggested departure but as she informed herself he was not the one to dictate what she could and could not do after all.

The steady motion of the ferry as it plodded its way across the narrow straits that divided the two close neighbours and provided a haven for wild life, coupled with the breeze that she allowed to torment her hair confident that with her new shorn locks she would easily be able to manage it, helped to lift her spirits from their dreary depth to new heights. Of course she had still the problem of the dining tables to sort out. This morning she was fortunate in that she had not seen either of her supposed companions but before the evening meal on board she determined that she would ask for a move somewhere else, for Helmut's remarks the previous evening had somewhat unnerved her. Her fingers rested against the weapon concealed under her clothes. In addition she had also this problem to sort out once and for all.

Glancing through the broad windows of the craft she spied groups of divers already manoeuvring through their tasks down in the ocean below and she couldn't help but wonder exactly where Gregg and Helmet had been planning on diving from and whether they had gone to the right place before she reminded herself that this had nothing at all to do with her providing they did not run into each other!

The more she thought about it the more she determined that with the airport close at hand this would make an ideal spot for Paul Butler to base himself if as she stipulated he was following the cruise at something of a distance because of something she did not fully appreciate. If that happened to be so it would also make an ideal spot to carry out the commission she had been handed and shoot the man. Divine Retribution for what he had done to her father as well as relieving British Intelligence of an agent they no longer desired working for them!

It was as the Island of Tenerife loomed larger on the horizon and the shores of La Gomera faded into the background that she glanced around the craft to view her fellow travellers that morning. Because of the hour there were not many on that boat, for the commuters anxious to start work in Tenerife had left much earlier and at the time it was far too early for any of the day visitors to think of returning. But as it was a tall well clad individual managed to catch her eye. She had a feeling that she had seen this person somewhere before and rapidly came to the conclusion that the woman like herself had managed to escape from the cruise liner to make an early start to the day. As it was the woman caught her looking in her direction and smiled back before she herself ventured to come across and speak to her.

"I am right, aren't I, you are from off the cruise ship as well?" Josie nodded finding herself engulfed in the other girl's beaming smile. "I thought that I was right but previously when I have seen you then you have been with your boy friend. So I presume this must be girls' day off today!"

"You have seen me with my boy friend?" For a moment Josie was puzzled and then realising to whom the girl was referring gave a laugh. "I can assure you that if you are speaking of Gregg then he definitely cannot be classified as my boy friend. He happens to be with his friend, they are a couple of marine biologists interested only in what lies under the waves not on top of them.

The fact of the matter is that by pure accident I happen to be sharing a table with them but that is as far as it goes. The name is Josie Craven by the way and you are --?"

"Fern Astor. I have also heard rumours that you are on television back home!"

"For my sins yes, I suppose that I am. But there again that is something I wish to forget about whilst I am on holiday. You are travelling on your own as well then?"

Fern nodded and for the first time Josie noticed the folder she was carrying under her arm.

"I'm sort of combining business with pleasure. The pleasure comes with the cruising but now we are in port I am afraid the business part comes into it!" She indicated her folder. "I guess I pride myself on being a bit of an artist and therefore I have taken the opportunity to bring one or two of my offerings over to Tenerife to take them to a couple of places I am familiar with, touristy spots, to see if they can use them!" She crossed her fingers hopefully.

"Then you are famous?"

"Certainly not as famous as what you are. I guess I'm sat with six old dears at meal times who can't stop talking about you every time you come into the restaurant. Not of course that they claim to watch you on television, it's always their grandchildren!" The two of them laughed out loud and Josie felt a real contact had been made with this girl. "Tell me are you crossing to Tenerife for anything special or are you simply going sightseeing?"

There was really no reply she could truthfully make to that. "Well I have never been to the place before but it seemed to be a lot more cosmopolitan than staying on La Gomera all day and besides I didn't really feel enamoured by spending the time listening to the native community corresponding by whistling to one another!"

"In that case if you are unfamiliar with Tenerife why not tag along with me for your first visit. I do happen to have a working knowledge of the area and once I have deposited my art forms we could perhaps spend part of the day together because for my part it will be a change to have a little feminine company of someone who is more of my own age. The old dears are really quite sweet but one can certainly have too much of them!"

"Why haven't you asked for a move?"

"I did but the head waiter told me he had no spaces available!"

"Well there are only three of us sitting at my table and if as a result this labels Gregg Anderson as being my boy friend then I would gladly welcome your company!" At least she mused Fern's presence at meal times should enable her to steer clear of that other pending conversation.

"You're sure you wouldn't mind?"

"Mind? I would welcome it. Just don't refer to my exploits on television, that's all. We will see this headwaiter and get things sorted when we get back if you like!"

"I do like it, but now we are coming into the port. Look you can see them all on the beach from here toasting themselves already. The sort of clientele who firmly believe that if they don't get burnt they won't get a suntan, and if they don't get that nobody will believe them when they say they have been on an exotic holiday!"

The two girls laughed at the idiosyncrasies of man as they left the ferry. Fern however was as good as her word and she certainly appeared to know that part of Tenerife and Josie felt extremely grateful she had met her for on her own she guessed she wouldn't have known where to start. Fern's business did not take long, for she had the bazaars she had intended to call at thoroughly mapped at and whilst Josie didn't consider any of her art work as being of sufficient quality for the standards of any art gallery she supposed that there was a place for them here where the general public appeared glad to mop up anything for presents to take home and souvenirs. That part of the business soon attended to, the girls then made to buy a coffee whilst they planned their next move and Josie's thoughts again turned to Paul Butler and the feeling she had that she might well find him here.

"I did hear that the airport in the south of the Island was situated not too far away from this resort?" Fern opened her eyes wide at this question.

"The airport? It is quite close I suppose, just at the back of the resort. But I didn't expect you to want to fill your time in here by visiting an airport that is much the same as any other?"

"No, forgive me, it was just something I heard about a friend catching a plane here and then catching transport into this resort!"

"Well many do use the bus from there. In fact the bus station is just across the road from here, but there are prettier sights to behold even in this place!"

"Of course, you a re my guide, it was simply curiosity on my part!" Her idea for spotting Paul Butler at this place was simply a pipe dream. "So where had you in mind to take me?"

"To show you the posh side of the place. It's not comprised solely of lager and bikinis you know. We'll make our way back to the shore and walk along a way. No doubt we will be able to pick up some lunch there as well before it is time for us to catch the ferry back less our transport leaves without us and we miss the focal point of the whole trip, the Cape Verde Islands!"

"You have been there before?" Fern shook her head.

"No although I have heard them termed as being the Islands of the New Caribbean that are situated at a far more manageable distance than their namesakes. Go, before it becomes too expensive, so I was informed! Is that the reason why you came on the cruise Josie?"

"I suppose it must have been. I've always been fascinated by place names anyway, although I must confess I have opted for the tours on the two Islands we drop anchor at!"

Fern nodded her head in agreement but by this time the girl's mind was full of their next activity of that particular day and not two days in the future and in spite of the sheer pleasure in walking past the more exclusive hotels of that place without reaching Los America's itself

Josie had a certain feeling that her quarry was even then close at hand.

The moment possibly came when they returned to the ferry itself for as the boat returned from the Island one figure departing from its decks sent her pulse racing. The sighting was by this time so unexpected that Josie merely gulped as the figure passed them by on the landing stage and for a moment she couldn't be positive that this was indeed Paul Butler, the one whom she sought and although the weapon she had brought pounded against her form by the time she had concluded that this figure was indeed him it was too late to do anything about it whereupon she chided herself yet again for her own ineptitude and concluded that she must indeed be proving to be totally inadequate in the eyes of the firm she now worked for.

"What's the matter?" Fern realised that her friend had stopped and was no longer following her onto the ferry.

"The man who got off just now. I have a feeling that I should know him!" Perhaps in all truth she should not have said anything to this person but then the other girl deserved some explanation.

"Well if he is just coming from off the boat then I'm afraid he has left it a little bit late for getting back. Whilst the crew are not exactly tyrants over such matters they are compelled to leave port at a predestined time. You were probably mistaken anyway for I saw no one that I recognised!"

"No doubt you are right!" Again she was forced to concede defeat.

"Well now for good measure we are getting on that craft for to leave it any later then we ourselves will be asking for a reprimand!"

"Of course!" Reluctantly Josie followed her noting that the sea had changed its colour from an azure blue to one with a more hidden depth.

"Surprisingly enough the tide does ebb and flow round here!" Fern had followed her eyes as Mount Teide receded into the distance and the forward panorama showed forth the welcoming arms of San Sebastian. "Remind me when we call at Santa Cruz on the way back to tell you about the pyramids. Not a lot of people who visit the Islands are aware of their existence and yet they are probably historically speaking at any rate one of the most important natural treasures that the Canaries can offer to us!"

Josie nodded, still not too convinced, her mind still hovering on what she considered to have been a lost opportunity. But the ferry was now entering the harbour at San Sebastian and even from this distance it was possible to discern two figures on the small promenade there waiting for their arrival.

"Looks as if we have company waiting for us!" Fern had assessed the situation with something of a cynical smile gracing her features. "Are you sure that one isn't your boy friend after all Josie? He looks as if he has been waiting for you and with the way he keeps looking in our direction and tapping his watch he must have thought we were in danger of missing the bewitching hour!"

Josie did not reply for at the time she was musing that if that had actually been Paul Butler leaving the ferry at the other side then he must have had some reason for visiting the two divers and of course she was not party to the answer to that puzzle!

"I did wonder whether you were going to make it!" It was Gregg who greeted Julie with something that could have been said to resemble a pout, almost indeed as if she had conspired to keep him waiting. Moreover by this time Fern had decided to make her escape and there was no sign of Helmut about either.

"Don't talk such rubbish, the boat isn't due to leave for ages yet!" For a moment she resented his interference.

In return he glanced at his watch pulling a face as he did so. "In that case I presume we have time for a drink at the Plaza before we board as I first intended?"

She glanced across at the area that he indicated where there was outside seating and a café area. In all truth she didn't particularly want to go for she would far rather have followed Fern back and boarded but the man was persistent. "Have you lost your friend then?" She screwed up her face.

"No, he sort of met someone he wanted to speak to and after that he was quite content to board. If you really want to know the truth He didn't really appreciate the fact that I wanted to wait for you!"

"Why did you then?" By this time however she had fallen into step with him heading towards that café.

"To make sure you got safely back on board of course!" He called the waiter over. "If it counts for anything I sort of missed you today!"

Snatches of conversation that had mistaken him for her boy friend flashed before her and almost simultaneously a blanket of cloud passed overhead blocking out the sun making her wonder if this sign was ominous or protective. Perhaps the answer came before they had finished their drink, for a sudden blustery shower drove them to take shelter under concrete rigging.

"I suppose you are going to blame that on me as well!" His expression could not help but make her smile. "Well that's better Miss Craven but I didn't think it would take the rain to make you finally smile!"

"The findings we have made today look promising!" Helmut Schmitz prided himself as he turned to his colleague earlier. "Of course we will need to compare the rock formation here with that of la Palma to satisfy ourselves that they were both formed through the same gigantic explosion even if some of the Islands did not immediate show themselves above sea level. All of which will give us more fuel to cement our theory on the lost city!" He looked justifiably pleased with himself so much so that Gregg began to wonder if this man ever thought of anything else outside of any Maritime task in hand. The answer he had conceded must be a positive no and his mind turned once again to that vexing female of whom they had caught no sight of that day and he wondered what she was up to. She hadn't gone on any of the recognised tours he was certain of that for the coaches had already returned and although occupied at the time with his own task he had kept an eye open for her. Well all he hoped now was that she was on that ferry coming across for he was positive that she had not remained on board after they had docked this morning. That was why his eyes were now firmly fixed on the craft as it drew closer to the spot where Teide could be viewed clouded in a skirt of mist and it was only when he saw her form emerging that Gregg Anderson allowed himself to relax.

"And you still insist that he isn't your boy friend?" Fern's eyes had opened wide at the man's greeting. But then she had hardly been convinced by Josie's fervent denials earlier on that day for hadn't the girl noticed them in the gardens at Reid's together on the previous day and they had appeared less than a couple of isolates at that time. In fact Fern now almost found it amusing to have this handsome creature who was still half clad in a divers outfit waiting to escort Josie back again to the ship almost as if he feared that unless he did she would make good an escape. That was the moment when Fern decided that the time had come for her to do a disappearing act.

Even so Josie herself however appeared non too pleased at this sort of interference. In truth she could not deny that Gregg had made an excellent companion and yet she was still determined not to get involved with him, which was probably the reason why she immediately went to sort out the headwaiter of the Restaurant on their return to see to it that Fern was placed on their table. At least she conceded, with this action she would have someone she could talk to at mealtimes and more importantly a situation that could not possibly be misconstrued. Not that the headwaiter wasn't flustered by these potential arrangements that appeared to have been made behind his back.

"Most unusual!" He muttered half under his breath. "I've never had that happen before! Not on any of the cruise ships I have sailed on anyway!"

"Well one supposes that there is always a first time for everything. As it is at the moment I am sat with two gentlemen without any female companion and there is also an empty place at our table!"

"But the people who the young lady has previous been sat with, won't they think such an arrangement reflects upon themselves?"

"If what Fern tells me is right then I don't suppose they will even notice that the girl is missing and anyway she was placed there rather outside of her age bracket!"

"And what of the two gentlemen already seated at the table you refer to, will they agree to another female presence?"

"I cannot really see why they should have any objection. After all they are together and seldom include me in their speech!"

Perhaps finally realising that this young lady would not give up her quest easily and not able to find any personal objection of his own, the headwaiter agreed albeit a little reluctantly. Consequently the boys were in for a bit of a shock at the evening meal that same evening when Josie ushered Fern to occupy the empty place at the table.

"Oh this is Fern Astor. Fern I might add happens to be an artist and someone with whom I have spent a gorgeous day on Tenerite today. We asked if she could be moved onto our table for we do have an empty place here and where she had initially been placed she found that she was bombarded on all sides with geriatrics. Hope you don't mind boys. By the way Fern meet Gregg and his diving partner Helmut!"

The greeting was solemn enough, Gregg obviously was the one who realised that perhaps there was more to the story behind Josie's reasoning than she cared to let on about although Helmut, after giving her a wan smile retreated into his world of what could possibly exist at the bottom of the ocean.

"So tell me have you had a successful day?" Sitting down Josie smiled across ignoring the face that Helmut was currently pulling. In actual fact what she wanted to know was whether Paul Butler had been there to see them and if so what he had wanted, but this was something she would have to try to find out for herself for there was no way she could actually put that question without revealing her own personal interest.

"Helmut was pleased with our findings from the dive, that is true, isn't it?" Gregg nudged his companion back into the present.

"Yes of course!" She knew that they were unlikely to get anymore from the Dutchman and therefore she presumed that this would be the end of the conversation therefore it came as something of a surprise when she heard Fern suddenly speak out.

"When the ferry came to pick us up a man got off it whom I believed I recognised from a way back. You didn't happen to see anything of Paul Butler over here did you?"

It was now Josie's turn to hang onto the other girl's words expectantly, wondering how on earth this person knew Paul Butler and also wondering now how the other two would respond to her question.

"I didn't realise that you knew Paul!" It was Gregg who was the one to reply. "As a matter of fact he came over to see how the diving was progressing as he just happened to be in the area and has always taken a keen interest in our work!"

"We sort of went out together for a time, oh I guess that was yonks ago because unfortunately that one was far too serious minded for me. So what is troubling you now Josie?"

The other girl made no response for far too many things were now preponderant in her mind!

At a time when Josie would well have preferred to be left on her own to bemoan the fact that she had proved to be an absolute failure in the task allotted to her, Fern had obviously other ideas. For before the meal was over the girl had not only stated her preference for going to a show that night but had also persuaded the others to dance in attendance to her wishes, a factor that surprised Josie for she had never associated Helmut in behaving in such a manner. Still the die was cast and therefore without being rude and calling off her attendance on some flimsy pretence she found that she was unwillingly accompanying them.

It was not that there was anything wrong with the show, in fact as shows go it was an excellent presentation, the cast working just as hard in that night's performance as they did on every occasion, it was simply that she needed to think for in the first place she had been given to understand that Paul Butler would be on board. At that stage her task had appeared simple, to follow him ashore and thus seek to meter out revenge for her father's death. But now she had discovered that not only was he not on board as a passenger but that he obviously had taken to visiting the ship when it was in port or at least some of the other passengers. And now the girl she had befriended also spoke of a past relationship with the man. It was time for her to think out a yet new strategy and that was not something that came to her easily as she gave her time to watching others prance around the stage.

Nor it appeared was Fern satisfied with simply sitting watching the show for afterwards she extolled the virtues of the dance floor to Gregg and found she had a willing listener in him. Even so she missed the look he passed in her direction when he took Fern's arm as laughing together they made towards the other salon. Thus it now seemed that she had been left with the long faced Helmut, a person who outside of diving did not appear able to arouse any sort of enthusiasm for anything. Thus to Josie's mind this promised to be a rather tedious evening.

Not so, for as she sat in silence with Helmut whilst the dancers strutted their stuff her back suddenly stiffened. Determined that she must now be elucidating Josie jumped to her feet in an attempt to follow the form that she had spotted as he retreated from the salon, her mind now unable to comprehend where this man had come from for after all hadn't they last seen him on the ferryboat going in the opposite direction to La Gomera? She had barely reached the door however when she felt the hand on her arm and realised that it was Gregg who had stopped her in her tracks.

"Now where do you think you are going? You're not trying to escape from the dance you promised me by any chance?"

Josie had no recollection of promising Gregg anything but the man was nothing if not determined and after glancing in vain after the retreating figure she found herself gently pulled back onto the dance floor, whilst Fern, who had so gallantly given up her partner, retreated back to entertain the unsuspecting Helmut.

"So what was the matter? Don't tell me that my little wallflower had tinges of jealousy because I was dancing with another partner and was therefore trying to retreat to the bar to drown her sorrows?" He had spun her round to face him as their steps moulded together.

"I just thought that I saw someone!" Begrudgingly she felt that she had to say something.

"Oh come off it Josie, I'm not falling for that one. You experienced a tinge of jealousy, admit it!"

"If that is what you want to hear O.K. I did then!" There was no point in arguing with the man and besides the shadowy figure that she thought she had seen had now disappeared completely out of sight.

"Well I can assure you that you needn't feel like that!" His eyes were now fixed upon her, as the music seemed to take over her senses. This was all that she needed. She had come here employed to do a job and all she had found was someone who could tug at will on her heartstrings! But then the music finished, it was time to return to the others.

"Did you see that man, I could have sworn ------!"? It was Fern who began and then immediately stopped probably realising her thoughts would have sounded too far-fetched. But then Josie could have sworn she had seen him too. Surely both of them couldn't have been wrong and yet to all intents and purposes the one whom she sought was not supposed to be travelling with them.

"You could have sworn what?" It was Gregg who took her words up to glean some sort of explanation

"This is positively silly but I could have sworn it was Paul Butler!" Now his expression became inscrutable whilst Josie was convinced that Helmut looked away quite deliberately. "And yet I know the man is not on board!"

"I take it that you know Paul Butler then?" In his questioning Gregg neither denied nor supported the girl's claim.

"I ought to know him. I went out with him at one time at what appears now to be a long time ago. Not for long because there was something about that person that

I felt I could not trust. But I would still be able to recognise his face!"

"Well you are right in saying that he is not on board, therefore perhaps you are suffering from hallucinations. Who knows maybe you are still hankering over the past!"

"Maybe!" Fern did not look too sure. Josie however was possibly more intrigued with the change in Gregg's attitude at mention of the man's name than anything else for the face of a potential lover had now turned cold and looked quite unforgiving and for once Josie was glad that she had kept her own feelings on the matter to herself. And yet the Dutchman still did not say anything, so much so that for a moment she wondered if he understood English, but that too was stupid reasoning on her part. Therefore from her point of view it seemed more advisable to say nothing at this stage on a happening that appeared to wreck the remainder of the evening for all of them!

Arising early the next morning after a rather restless night during which time her mind had actively pondered over the relevant facts Josie found she was in time to join the Thai Ching exercises on the sundeck before breakfast. Exercises that vainly promised to keep your weight down despite overindulgence in the never-ending mass of delicates that were offered on board and which one found very hard to refuse. She had only just joined in when she was conscious that he was watching her now with a wry smile on his face and looking for all the world as if he was ready to come out with some cryptic comment at her expense. The mood from the previous evening had now all disappeared to be replaced with one of a friendlier disposition and perhaps because she made no effort to break off from her exercises, he made to join her.

"Well I suppose this is the only way that I can manage to have a conversation with you!" He complained good naturedly to be frowned upon by the trainer in charge for spoiling the silence she had insisted upon. And as the man had no intention of giving up his quest Josie realised that the only way one could achieve some form of humanity was for her to drop out.

"I won't apologise I could already tell that you'd had enough!" He cheekily purported his excuse as they left the area together. "Actually I did want to find you on your own to apologise about last night. It was totally wrong of me to behave in that manner when Fern mentioned Paul Butler, but the fact of the matter is that one has been rather a thorn in the side. He is supposed to be interested in the diving but has taken to following Helmut around wherever he goes hoping, one presumes to glean some information about his finds from him. He was the person you saw on the ferryboat for he had just been over to La Gomera to chat up Helmut once again. Not that he was for telling him anything, well actually there is nothing to tell at the moment, so when Fern said that she thought she had seen him on the boat I simply saw red. Quite wrongly I admit with two ladies present but more especially because I didn't want you to take offence!" He took a breath of the clear morning air. "So now in the cool light of day, am I forgiven?"

"I suppose that is a consideration!"

"Good, and as it is far too early yet to contemplate breakfast, now we are friends again let's go and watch the waves tormenting the bow of the ship and see the sun rise up out of the ocean. A special sight I believe, evident only in these climes!"

She supposed it was the view where she found her new found solace from for there were no other ships to disturb them across the horizon only the white foam of the waves that created patterns across the wake of the vessel. Patterns so regular that one could easily have been hypnotised by them in the wake of their constant song. But hypnosis was not something that Gregg wanted. Instead he wanted them to plan out that day at sea together so that they could please themselves instead of listening to the dictates of others.

"But what about Fern?" She suddenly felt anxious about her new friend, almost indeed as if she was deserting her.

"No doubt Fern will have her own plans. Don't forget she had been on the boat for some time before you found her and the idea was for her to share a table, not our lives! You said that she was an artist I believe?"

"Yes, that was the reason why I met her. She was crossing on the same ferry to peddle some of her wares at some predestined locations and as she was quite familiar with Los Christianos and I was not, I sort of tagged along, which proved rather beneficial as far as I was concerned!"

"Interesting I suppose. Did she show you any of this art work then?"

"Actually no she didn't, but the parcels were all wrapped up so I suppose she didn't feel like undoing them. Anyway she said she wasn't famous or anything like that!" Josie pouted, she thought they had finally got away from discussing other people

Still breakfast was to prove a far more light-hearted affair and the other two participants had as Gregg had suspected, already sorted out their own day. Consequently after a brief respite it was the swimming pool where Gregg and Josie headed. If she thought it strange that a diver would want to spend his time off in this sort of activity she was soon to be proved wrong for this was something that Gregg could relax whilst participating and then after towelling themselves dry and changing into shorts it was the deck that once again beckoned. By this time some of the decks were quite crowded with inhabited deck chairs and waiters running around to obey their occupants every command, but there were other places that were semi deserted, possibly because the clientele preferred to roast rather than to feel the wind on their features and this was the obvious place for the two of them to gravitate towards.

Lounging on the deck with the wind blowing through her hair as the ship throbbed its way forward across the ocean, Josie eyed the white sea horses and wondered if they were trying to impart some message with words caught up in the Atlantic breeze where the morning sun now beat down completely enshrouded by this time with cloud. It was whilst she was in this position that his words reached her ears

"So tell me something. How come you arrived on this cruise when your prime intention was initially to traverse the Rhine valley in the hope of meeting someone?"

"I thought I told you, my contact wasn't there and I got a message from the people I work for that a place had been reserved for me on this cruise. Not that I wasn't more than a little perturbed at the time but as things have turned out it is a brilliance I never expected!"

"So it was the television people who persuaded you to come on this cruise. But why, was it because they wanted to get rid of you, replace your character?"

"Far from it, I actually took leave of absence from the set promising that they could write me in when I got back. But didn't I tell you all this before?"

"You probably did, but if you are not currently working for the television people who are you employed by that throws in a cruise for good measure?"

"Just a place called Locations!" There was no way on earth she was confessing her true motives to him whatever she was beginning to think about him. "I suppose one could call it an off shoot from the television in that the firm look for places suitable for filming in the future so that when the time comes they won't be fishing around with no new ideas!"

"Then you must have been lucky or indeed fortunate to be selected in that capacity?"

"Neither, you see I had just lost my father in rather tragic circumstances, made all the worse because there were things I needed to say to him but never got the chance, so I suppose feeling they could do little with me at the time they decided to send me on this!"

They looked up as Fern holding an artist board of some description passed them by without obviously seeing them. "Well obviously we have not upset Fern by choosing to do our own thing, which is what I told you in the first place. Still I guess you landed on your feet when you got this job. Are you sure you had no one pulling the strings for you?"

"No one, and now it is your turn Gregg Anderson. I left you expecting you to be going to Amsterdam remember?"

"I did only to find Helmut was fired up about going on this cruise with all his undersea maps and so forth. Still the way that things have turned out I can't say that I'm sorry. Who knows maybe he is right after all and we will make some phenomenal break through and find his lost city. I still doubt it very much myself, for the waters that surround that supposedly hidden place are far too deep for mere divers. But I suppose the thought of it keeps our Helmut happy and at the same time I have managed to find myself a very affable companion! Therefore who could possibly ask for more?"

She felt her face flushing as he regarded her with that pair of dark luminous eyes and noticing her expression he laughed. "All right, I suppose that is enough torment for one day but no doubt I will be back for more. I believe there is a lecture come film show all about our next port of call currently available. Interested?"

She nodded her head unable to think of what else to do but decided that this was probably the better of two evils. There was still so much that she didn't understand, on top of which she now felt her heart melting at the sight of this man. All of this was something she could well have done without for she was getting no closer to completing the task she had vowed to complete and had taken the Queen's shilling for.

Chapter Five

The fact that a new passenger had boarded the ship at La Gomera possibly came as something of a surprise to Josie for after all that was not a recognised boarding place. That was however until she remembered the other passenger who had disembarked with luggage earlier on in the day. The even greater surprised was however when Josie realised just who this newcomer was. Her initiation moreover happened in quite an accidental manner.

Fern herself had departed for a course being held on landscape painting on one of the middle decks and therefore drifting up to the Observation lounge herself in an attempt to relax her mind listening to some lunchtime melodies she was more than a little surprised when one of the suite doors on the same level as this lounge opened and a certain person stepped out. It was a surprise however that turned into something like shock as she realised that she recognised this person for indeed unless she was very much mistaken this represented the form of Baron Aldermatt, the mysterious character from the

Lorcley valley whom she had once had the misfortune to meet.

A shiver accosted her spine as she remembered the way he had greeted her on their last meeting at the Gasthaus. This time Maria was not here to come to her rescue and consequently she tried desperately to slink up the companion way fervently hoping that this man had not noticed her; the thought of what he was doing here on this cruise not at the time occurring to her. Alas however it appeared that she was too late to escape unnoticed for a moment later she felt his hands resting on her shoulders and she was left to ponder upon what sort of coincidence this could be!

"Ah now I do believe it is the delightful Fraulein Craven. I hadn't expected our paths to cross again so soon my dear!" Josie cringed as she realised that it was too late to escape.

"It is quite a surprise to see you here on this cruise Baron!" She desperately tried to calm her trembling lips.

"Oh I have some minor business matter to attend to that required my presence in Mindelo. Initially I did consider flying there direct but then I decided that perhaps a sea voyage would suit my constitution far better which is something that I must whole heartedly agree with especially after noting your own presence here, for if I remember correctly we never did have the opportunity to conclude our conversation. Still maybe you will tell me what brings you on such a voyage? You do not appear to be still grieving, therefore perhaps if we share a coffee together you will satisfy my curiosity. That is unless you prefer something stronger?"

"No thank you Baron, I guess a coffee will suit me fine!" There was now no point in arguing with this person who appeared to have her at a definite disadvantage.

Consequently she was soon to find herself facing the Baron across the sumptuous furnishings of the Lounge, where through the massive windows at the front of the boat, the tide heralded its presence in a tantalising fashion in an attempt to lure the unsuspecting to step into its blue inviting mass to pay homage to King Neptune.

"I believe you were visiting our beautiful valley in the Rhine as a result of your father's tragic death Miss Craven?" Obviously the view of the blue waters was not what was holding the man's interest at the time.

She nodded in response for it appeared pointless to argue and there appeared to be no way of escaping the talons of this creature whilst they were afloat.

"Ah yes! Your father visited my castle on several occasions prior to his death. I always considered the man to be most knowledgeable and I was most upset when I heard of his unfortunate demise. But then I believe you came to the Rhine initially to learn more about his accident. Surely that cannot be related to the fact that you are now here on this cruise.

Josie opened and closed her lips several times for words currently failed her for there was literally no way by which she could explain her reason for her current venue. Yet even as she was still pondering on her words of response a certain familiar voice hastened to come to her rescue.

"Oh my fiancé came so that she could accompany me on a business venture!"

The words that were uttered obviously jarred upon the Baron even more than what they jarred on Josie as she looked up into the eyes of the one claiming to be her fiancé. Still she argued with herself that after all Gregg meant no harm by his words, he was merely trying to come to her assistance and therefore she managed to smile rather benignly back in his direction.

"They do say Baron that man finds it difficult without having a partner to back him up!"

"Then it appears that congratulations are in order. Still as it happens we do have forty eight hours before we are due to arrive in Mindelo and therefore I am sure you will be able to find it in your heart to spare an old man a little of your valuable time Miss Craven for if you remember I said that I knew your father well and that he was a frequent visitor to my castle. Therefore perhaps you feel that you owe that much to his memory?"

"Sorry but as my fiancé is also acting as my secretary we have actually rather a tight schedule to meet!"

"And you are?" The Baron was obviously still impressed as he took in Gregg's form.

"Gregg Anderson. I am a marine biologist!"

"Ah so I take it that you catch fish so that the girl here can utilise her time measuring them?"

"Not true. You see there are many other things that concern a marine biologist such as the shifting seasons and the consequent affect on the natural habitat!"

Still mesmerised by Gregg's intervention Josie had no idea whether the Baron believed this rhetoric and yet she felt extremely grateful to this man who now appeared to be monopolising a large part of her life and yet the terminology he had used when he had called her his fiancé she hardly thought was necessary. For his part however, after one last penetrating glance in her direction at least seemed to be willing to escape from the situation. "Well there are still many things I would like to tell the girl about her father but I suppose they will suffice for another time." He was obviously not going to press his point any further at that stage and as the Baron turned to go Gregg gave a whoop of delight at what he considered to be a feat of success.

"Well after that little performance I consider that my fiancé owes me at least a kiss!"

She turned her cheek in his direction but this act was obviously not enough for Gregg who moved her face and placed his lips upon her own. It was pointless for her to resist and in point of fact Josie did not want to for there was something that felt strangely comforting in their lips meeting even if her emotions appeared in something of a turmoil.

"Guess I thought that this would happen!" His lips moved only to whisper the words and remained situated still dangerously close to her own. "But perhaps now you will tell me why you chose to hide yourself away up here in the first place. You wouldn't have been running away from anything would you?"

"That is nonsense! If you must know Fern appears to be occupied with her water colours and I didn't want to inflict myself on you and Helmut for the pair of you appeared to be busy. Besides I have the distinct impression that Helmut doesn't like me all that much!"

"Now you are talking rubbish, of course Helmut likes you. Not as much as what I do of course and I must admit that the man is so obviously steeped in his science that he often gives the wrong impression. But I wanted to find you for there is a port lecture on this afternoon about our next port of call Mindelo. I thought you would be interested!"

Josie remembered seeing it listed on the Ship's Times and realised she had forgotten about it, therefore she cast a smile in his direction. "Of course I am interested!"

"Then let's go then. It's in the Neptune lounge apparently!"

Things did not get any easier for Josie when they went to this meeting however for the most unexpected was about to happen. The ship's officer who was in charge of leisure activities had made his opening spiel when he quite suddenly decided to introduce a person he deemed was much better qualified to speak about the Islands than he was himself. Yet it was Josie who let out the first gasp when she saw whom this person was. It was a gasp that was echoed by her companion for the one in question was most definitely in the likeness of Paul Butler. Josie's immediate thoughts were that this justified her own sightings of the man on the boat the previous day although it was impossible to glean what Gregg was thinking at that time. Still the man currently stationed on the podium spoke eloquently and he appeared to be quite knowledgeable about their next port of call at Mindelo, which was on one of the twenty Islands that made up the archipelago in the Southern Atlantic. It was only once he had finished his spiel that both of them moved forward, almost of one mind, in an attempt to delay this person. But even this action appeared to be fraught with its own set of difficulties for after taking a limited amount of questions the man concerned glanced at his watch and then was gone like some willo' the wisp in the night.

"Then we did see him ---He is on the boat after all!" It was Josie who was able to voice her feelings the first as she sat there by this time feeling an absolute failure in the assignment that had been allotted to her. Gregg's lips at that time appeared to be tightly closed almost as if a thousand thoughts were also propounding on his nervous system. When he finally spoke however his words were nevertheless to surprise her.

"Guess I'll have to tell Helmut about this. He is not going to credit the man with being here!" Josie looked at the one issuing forth this sentiment as if she could not believe her ears. Her own initial inclination had been to tell Fern for after all she considered that it was this girl who had been humiliated simply by her stating that she had seen this same person on the previous evening and yet something was halting her from doing that! Maybe it was basic instinct and yet now Gregg would have none of it.

They eventually found the other two in one of the reading rooms, together but strictly apart, Helmut confined to looking up his charts and Fern who had finished her art class now handling her sketchpad as if she had just received some divine inspiration on some subject matter. It was of course Helmut whom Gregg made towards to break his news although in truth his voice was able to carry so that the other girl missed little of the conversation.

"You don't even appear surprised!" Gregg finally finished his rendition with a note of chastity that the other had taken the news without showing any mental disturbance.

"Should I be? After all the man is a free agent and I have no doubt he is knowledgeable on his subject matter!"

"But what of the fact that he is on this boat after all we said?"

"Probably he is earning his passage by giving lectures which will save him having to fork out for an air fare!"

"Then you expected to see him at our next port of call?"

"All things are possible. I know that he appeared enthused with what we were about!"

Josie noticed that Fern for one had remained very quiet during this conversation. Initially she supposed she had expected the girl to have jumped up and defended her previous statement that she had spotted the man on the previous day and moreover Josie could tell simply by looking at Fern's expression that she had heard the conversation, which had, it could be stated, have hardly held any claim to being suppressed.

Even so before she was granted any opportunity of questioning the girl about the matter the most unexpected happened! And this was to come in the form of an emergency cacophony of sound, which appeared to emanate in a series of blasts from the ship's funnel. She remembered that there had not been any practise drill held on board that vessel when they had first left port, which was the usual custom and whether the crew, now realising their unforgivable mistake were trying to rectify matters in a way that they considered would alleviate some of the boredom that the several days voyaging without making port and now afflicting the passengers, would surely bring remained a matter for conjecture. What did happen was that there was an immediate mass exodus from all activities currently taking place with all participants dashing around and wondering in which direction they should go. The fact that such emergency directions had been pasted in their cabins along with individual lifebelts was apparently a trivial matter that had obviously escaped their attention and consequently the ship's crew had their work cut out in trying to contain this mass of folk all talking and shouting at once and guide them to the right stations.

It was only an exercise and profuse apologies were later broadcast from the Captain in respect of one individual who would remain nameless, who had actually motivated the wrong switch up on the fore deck. Thus with all sense of impending danger now removed the passengers at least began to relax and began to make a loud noise refusing to clear the gangways until they had exerted all their chatter. It was therefore some time before things settled back down to normal and it was during this time that Josie at last spotted Fern whose emergency station was situated not far from her own. Still it did not appear that Fern had joined the rest of her companions with the sense of worry now alleviated from their faces.

"What's the matter?" It was now easy for Josie to manoeuvre her way over to the girl as she still stood on the deck.

"I'm convinced I saw that person again during the drill, he was in a cluster not far away from my own!"

"He was also lecturing in the salon earlier this morning!" Josie had been convinced that the girl already knew this but now a morning newspaper she held in her hand seemed to focus in on her argument. "Didn't you hear Gregg telling Helmut about it?"

"Have you seen this morning's headlines?" Fern made no attempt to answer the question. Instead she pushed the newspaper into Josie's hands.

"What, you mean you are referring to this recent Anglo French agreement concerning military hardware?" Josie spoke the words quite convinced that she must have got hold of the wrong end of the stick but these were the headlines in the mornings' newspaper to which the girl had been referring.

"Yes, probably at a most inopportune time as well I would suggest!"

"Sorry, but I guess you have lost me on that one. I know that some remarks have been passed against such a liaison, but with the economic clime being what it is, surely it is one way we can be sure of protecting our sovereign strategy!"

"You think so? Then perhaps your naïvety is to be admired Josie even if such ideas cannot really be substantiated. I am thinking now of outside influences that could easily see their way into using this to achieve their own ends!"

"And I think you are reading far more into the matter than was ever intended. All of which points to the fact that it is high time we went and got ourselves a coffee to recover from this shindig that has just erupted in front of us!"

The girl said no more which left Josie feeling even more puzzled. In all honesty she had come to inform Fern of the sighting of one Paul Butler and had now found her companion to be more embroiled in British politics. And how all that fitted in with Fern claiming to be an artist was quite another matter!

"I guess you found your friend again?" It was Gregg who caught up with them as they entered the place where they could secure their coffee and Fern had moved over to the serving hatch to do exactly that.

"Yes, although strangely enough she seems to be more concerned with today's newspaper headlines than she does with the justification of her sightings of Paul Butler, or the fact that the man happens to be on board!"

"A matter that appears to have quickly gravitated you away from your own interest in seeking out the man. You have never told me yet why you wanted to travel up into the Rhine to meet him in the first place!"

"It was a private matter!" Again Josie found herself on the defensive.

"Surely not a clandestine meeting. I never thought of you as having a secret lover before!"

"Most definitely not!"

"And yet you are still not for confiding in me. What is it then a question of trust then?"

"No, it is a question of what I owe to others outside of myself and to their memory. Sorry but I am not prepared to say anymore on the subject!"

"Then it strikes me that if Paul Butler happens to be on this boat, which we both now know that he is, this ought to afford you a splendid opportunity to get off your chest what it is that you want to say to this man. I was willing to offer my support on the matter but apparently that does not appear to be required!"

"I still don't get why Fern is so tied up with this Anglo–French business!" Again she was attempting to change the subject.

"Perhaps she feels it might interfere with the sale of her art work! Oh why ask me, I really have no idea, ask her yourself she is heading back with the coffee!"

Nothing further having been resolved after that impromptu coffee break, Gregg resolved that he must see what Helmut was up to following the practise alarm. "Come to think of it I never even spotted him on deck with his life belt so in all probability the man is still immersed in his maps!" She wondered then whether this was an excuse to leave the other two but as Fern appeared to have recuperated fully by this time and was now immersed with her canvas, Josie decided to follow him. In a way she supposed it was the lesser of the two evils. She reasoned that she could have taken such an opportunity to seek out Paul Butler but she could never have committed the task set out for her to do in such restricted confines of a boat. No the only way was to wait until this man was ashore and alone at some point. Mind you she also began to wonder whether she was indeed beginning to look for excuses, but then merely thinking of her father and the opportunity she had lost to speak to him in later years strengthened her resolve.

Neither, she admitted was she going to get any change out of Fern for the woman had accepted the present rationale by drawing furiously on that board. Josie's basic instincts had been to attempt to see what the woman was currently occupied with, but this indeed proved to be a step too far for the woman had once again crept beneath the cloud of sympathy. Therefore Josie made her own excuse to herself that she would probably get far more out of following Gregg than staying on her own.

Nevertheless she was more than a little surprised when the man on his way to rejoin his friend stopped by at the Bridge House to have a word with the Captain. She was even more surprised when she realised that the two men also appeared to get on fine. Not that she supposed there was anything unusual in that for the Captain was an affable fellow it was just that Gregg's timing appeared to be all wrong. Still any questions she would have liked to pursue on that score seemed to once again be pushed into the background especially when she viewed the other two speaking so earnestly together. Helmut as was the norm had the map he was referring to now placed down on the table and now it appeared that he was pointing out various places to Gregg.

"It is possible that we should be able to collect some micro-organisms from this region. If I am correct they should provide a useful comparison to those we managed to get from further North and at least provide us with some idea as to whether these came from the same source in rock formation or whether these Islands are entirely divorced from their counterparts further North!"

"And what of the other? Have you consulted with him? If so what did he have to say on this matter?"

"As a matter of fact he agrees with me. Fortunate in a sense that he is travelling with the boat so that we can get any formal liaison's out of the way: Unfortunate however in the sense that you still have that girl hanging round. For his own reasons Butler objects very much to her presence, which I suppose under the circumstances is not surprising. I accept that he claims to have had nothing to do with her father's death but even so she is well capable of making a damned nuisance of herself. In addition there is also the presence of the other one, the artist, the waif and stray that the girl managed to pick up when she was let off the leash!"

"I presume he objects to her presence as well?"

"The trouble he says is that nobody knows anything about her and that my friend is something that he doesn't like!"

"But she is some sort of artist. Josie said that she was peddling her wares on Tenerife and anyway she claims that she once went out with Butler!"

"Can we be certain about that? It appears to be a rather flimsy story; at least it does to my ears. No something is wrong, we appear to be lampooned by unfathomable females this time around and that is not what we initially planned!"

"Well I admit that Fern appears to take an interest in world news if that is what you are inferring. I even caught Josie questioning her on that!"

"There, you are mentioning that girl's name yet again. I thought I had already made it quite clear that this project is for us alone and we do not need her tagging along!"

"She has her own motives for being on this voyage!"

"Yes, to trace Paul Butler. But then she has already achieved that now so why is she still here?"

"Possibly because the ship is unlikely to stop and put her ashore in the midst of these waters!"

"Then do me a favour Anderson. In fact do the cause a favour and drop her. In fact drop both of them. One is enough to cause trouble, but the two combined together could be fatal!"

He broke off suddenly as if realising that the conversation, which he had deemed to be private was being overheard and both men now looked up in her direction as if fearing a following onslaught after their words. But Josie remained silent mainly because a state of complete shock had now enveloped her. It now appeared that the men had already realised her motivation and consequently she questioned herself as to whether she had truly behaved as an employee of that prestigious Government branch or whether she had been lax in her mannerisms thus giving others the opportunity to question. Perhaps even now it was Gregg who fully realised her predicament and came across to speak to her.

"Let's face it Josie we admit we all know Paul Butler, one could say that as Marine biologists he is an acquaintance of ours. But Helmut's interest still lies in his subject matter, believe it or not and Paul Butler once was a very good amateur diver. In fact Helmut in his way often asks why the man ever gave it up for he said that he was becoming quite good at the sport!" He shrugged his shoulders as he realised that Josie still appeared dubious.

"Perhaps the time has come to question what is it that you hold against the man for there is little need for anyone to question your motives Josie for you see I am afraid your identity was a foregone conclusion even before you sct foot on this boat!"

" I don't suppose you would consider them to be really important. It is simply that this man Paul Butler happened to murder my father!" There the words were out before she could bite them back, she had stated her case and she waited for their rejoinder.

In turn Gregg whistled. "I suppose I find it a little difficult to tell you that you must have got your facts wrong Josie, but you happen to have the wrong guy to resort to anything like that!"

Josie shook her head. She had a job to complete and no one, not even Gregg was going to dissuade her from this task

"O.K let's change the subject. A little while back you spoke of your father's effects being given to you. I believe you mentioned that they contained a map?"

"Did I?" Josie didn't need to pretend that she had no recollection of saying anything of the kind and how Gregg Anderson happened to know about it remained a mystery to her. "I know that my father was interested in maps in his life, especially puzzling ones!"

"And one such map was passed onto you along with your father's other effects?"

Josie pulled a face. The moments spent with Gregg Anderson were now well and truly over if indeed they had ever existed in the first place. But if his kindness to her had been merely a ploy to get his hands on this particular map then he was very much mistaken.

"There were several items so I bundled them altogether but I know nothing of any map. But tell me why are you suddenly so interested?"

"Perhaps you are unaware of Helmut's prize dream and apparently your father did possess a map that suggested the possible location of the lost city of Atlantis!"

"If that is the case then I am afraid that I know little about it!" She felt her knees beginning to shake but all she knew was that she wanted this conversation to finish but by this time Helmut himself had approached them.

"I believe you think that Paul Butler was the one to kill your father? Well on that madam you are totally wrong. It was indeed your own father who attempted to assassinate Paul Butler and the man was killed as a result of an accident, an action that had nothing to do with Butler I must add!"

She felt her hands now feeling for that weapon and then realised with wearing her shorts she had not put the harness on. Some sort of agent she was making, she reproved herself and then shaking herself alive entered fully into the defence of her father arguing that the others were totally wrong in their assumptions.

"Then if you will not believe us perhaps you ought to question Paul Butler for yourself and please remember this is not some fictitious plot that you have been handed to act out!"

"I have no intention of asking that man anything although I would dearly like to know of your own involvement in this case!"

"The answer to that is far more simple. Gregg and I are first and foremost scientists, marine biologists as a matter of fact in case that information has previously escaped you. Our main interest lies in trying to discover the truth about the reported claims of the lost land of Atlantis lying somewhere deep in the ocean in these parts. That is why we are in the process of collecting fossils and other samples from various locations for comparison and analysis, for if such an almighty eruption occurred that was enough to consequently bury the existing landmass under some tsunami; then it is highly probable that debris from such an event was deposited over a large area. That is our reason for being here Miss Craven, now what of your own?"

"If I said it was to kill the man responsible for my own father's death, what would you say to that?" She hated her confession for this was beyond her brief to reveal such motives but in truth the man had got her all charged up and what was more he knew it!

"Then I would enquire if you are a British citizen why you feel it necessary to wreak your vengeance on one of Her Majesty's servants who could be found guilty only on the count of acting in self defence?"

The very suggestion that her own father had been the perpetrator now acted to rile up the gall within her. "I think I have based my argument on very good professional advice and therefore I totally disagree with your presumptuous statement!"

"In that case why don't you ask the man in question to relate his side of the story and then perhaps you will get some inkling of how far you are wrong in your diagnosis!"

"I have no intention of doing any such thing!" Disdainfully she made to move away. Gregg would have followed but Helmut stayed him.

"Let her be for the moment for I believe there is another who could prove to be far more dangerous to our cause than Miss Craven. I am speaking now of the person who calls herself Fern Astor who has now laid claim to being on the periphery of our activities. I for one would like to know exactly what she is carrying in those packages she distributes around. Of one thing I feel certain and that is that they are not innocent pieces of art. She is the one whom we need to watch. As far as Miss Craven is concerned I have no doubt that I can leave her case in the hands of my lady's man. Yes, I know that you are attracted Gregg, well now use that attraction you obviously feel for the opposite sex in a constructive manner!" Helmut picked up his maps indicating yet again that the conversation was now over and he desired no more disturbances at that time and Gregg was therefore left to wonder where Josie had now taken it in her head to disappear to.

For her part, still feeling furious with herself for giving away so much information, Josie had gone in search of Fern, who had now chosen to disappear again and moreover was a girl who proved at the time to be non too easy to find and when Josie finally did trace her she found her much to her surprise outside of the purser's office

"Just a ship to shore call I needed to make!" The other girl smiled obviously guessing her thoughts. "I just wanted to know if I had any more responses requesting my art work whilst I was out here. You see if that was the case then it would have saved me some considerable postal charges when I returned to the U.K.!"

"And had you had any enquiries then?" To Josie's mind the girl must indeed have something of a business head on her shoulders if she could undertake this sort of work whilst on holiday.

"One or two actually, which will coincide with our return back to the Canaries after paying our respects to the Cape Verde Islands. Something that is rather beneficial in a way because it will afford me some further time to complete them!" She laughed as if she had passed some joke tossing her hair over her shoulder in a rather nonchalant manner. "Stop looking so disapprovingly at me Josie, after all enterprise is the name of the game. But if I might say something you appear a little despondent, and that is a something that I thought non existent as far as you were concerned!"

"Perhaps I have just been subjected to a difference of opinion!"

"And that I gather is something that you find hard to come to terms with. It would be a pleasant life indeed if one did not come across those in a lifetime but on the other hand such an existence would probably prove to be most boring!"

"It concerned the person who goes by the name of Paul Butler!" At least she now had the satisfaction of seeing the girl's expression change, this time into one of more sombre reflection. In truth she had no idea why this mention should have had such an effect on Fern for apart from seeing him from a distance on several occasions Josie was under the impression that any relationship that had existed between the two of them was well in the past. Still she supposed that one could consider Fern herself to be something of an enigma and she still mused on the real contents of the ship to shore telephone messages. Nothing it appeared on this trip was going to prove to be straightforward and all that she desired was to complete this mission as soon as possible and leave the rest of them to it!

Still deep in her thoughts at what had transpired Josie supposed it was within her nature to seek to befriend that solitary figure whose only task upon that boat appeared to be attending to the closets on the Lounge Deck for in truth she had already heard about his own tragic story and perhaps this fact helped to soothe her own thoughts at the time. Born a Philippino and the eldest of nine children he had been forced to seek work after the tragic demise of his parents in order to support his brothers and sisters. Yet whilst the young man was charming and well-mannered Josie had spied the look of sadness held in his eyes as he went about completing his tasks and consequently it was no surprise when she sought him out to speak to him. New to his work the young man was possibly unaware of the gentler side of the British spirit and appreciating that someone should find the time to speak to him he related back on yet another matter that had troubled him.

"The two men I saw on Deck nine. One I am sure was carrying a knife. I thought that he was going to attack the older man who had his back turned away at the time, but then he spotted me and slipped the weapon away. Now I do not know whether I should report this matter for they may believe that it is a figment of my imagination and if they do then I will lose my job for it is not my place to bring any judgement upon the passengers on this ship!"

"But if what you saw is true then the matter ought to be reported!" Josie responded without heed to the weapon she was carrying and the task she was determined to complete. "But tell me can you describe the two men who were involved?"

"One of them was a large dark haired man, I do not think that he was English for I heard him speak and the voice it had an accent. The other man, the one with the knife, I think that he was English; he was tall with fairish hair. I think that both men they boarded the boat at La Gomera when some other passengers disembarked!"

"Then I do think you ought to tell someone about it!" Josie's mind froze as she remembered exactly who had boarded the boat at La Gomera. But this matter could not go unreported. Yet the young man still looked hesitant. "Would you like me to go along to the purser with you?"

He returned a grateful smile of thanks taking off his gloves in readiness. Yet as they reached the door to the outside someone else was stood there ready to intervene.

"I suppose you realise that you are quite likely to give him a false impression of the English. Not all members of our nation are quite as kind hearted as what you appear to be!" Gregg was scathing as he saw her in the presence of the Philippino. Why he had followed her there she had no idea but seeing them together the man had obviously got the wrong impression.

"I had presumed that our conversation earlier was finished!" She tried her best to make her tone clip but found this was not easy. Meantime obviously embarrassed her young friend was now seeking to make an escape. "No don't go Vernon, our business is of some importance!" She stalked ahead of the Philippino leaving him to trail behind and leaving Gregg in something like a state of turmoil!

★ ★ ★ ★

Chapter Six

It was not until they were actually treading the deck that Josie realised that a strong wind had suddenly sprung up. Possibly in her desire to indict Paul Butler she had not previously noticed it but now it caused her to sway whilst the young Philippino looked back at her in dismay. On reflection however perhaps it was not the fact that she swayed that caused the young man's anxiety but rather the fact that he had noticed perhaps for the first time that they were now being followed. Thus as Gregg's arms moved out almost automatically to support her the young Philippino decided to take the opportunity to make good his own escape for the young man valued his job more than anything else and reporting matters concerning a passenger would have earned him no favours.

Yet even as Gregg drew her closer to him more than one question was now manifesting itself in his eyes. "Don't even try to argue your way out of this one Josie, what exactly are you up to now?"

She shrugged her shoulders in a disparaging manner at him. "If you must know that young man has just witnessed an altercation on one of the upper decks and I believe it concerned Paul Butler with someone else that I believe I know!"

"Then take my advice and forget it, for after all the young man appeared keen to do exactly that. As a matter of fact I expect he respects his job far too much to become involved in any argument. Anyway for what it is worth I don't suppose things were as bad as you imagined, which then brings me to my second question which is simply if you are querying the prospect of weapons being used on board then why have you not yet parted with the weapon you are carrying? I know full well that it is not really your style for I have observed that every time you have passed through customs I have seen you looking jumpy. In fact how you have got away with carrying that weapon so far I guess I will never know. You must lead a charmed existence that is all that I can say!"

"I carry it for a purpose!" She didn't know how on earth he had reached the conclusion that she was carrying the gun but her lips remained taut as she spit out her response.

"Then just supposing that the purpose you wear it for is no longer valid?"

"That is totally fallacious talk. My father was killed by one certain person and that same person is currently with us here on this boat remember?"

"So that is why you were keen to support the young man when he deemed to have seen this person with a weapon on the upper deck? And to think that all this time I was given to understand that your father died as a result of an accident!"

"I couldn't care less who told you that but I can assure you it was no accident otherwise why would I would have been subsequently commissioned to carry out this task!"

Gregg shrugged. "Perhaps it is time that you started to accept the truth of what really happened Josie. But if there is still the slightest form of doubt in your mind let me try to wipe out such doubts in stages. You could make a start by showing the map your father left to Helmut!"

"Why?"

"Because maybe that will help at least to start to unravel a little of this fairy tale for you!"

This man, she decided somewhat bluntly must have sort of a hypnotic influence over her for Josie found herself obediently returning from the safe in her cabin with the maps in question in her hand ready to seek out Helmut who was still in the library. As she entered whilst still not knowing whether she was indeed doing the right thing she noticed the person whom she sought looking up questioningly in her direction. That was indeed her cue to commence unfolding the map in question and finally laying it out on one of the tables.

For a few minutes Helmut studied the document before his face adopted a more serious expression as he looked up at her rather searchingly. "Where did your father get this map from?" Even so despite his question she had to admit that the tone sounded decidedly more cordial.

"I guess he was simply a collector, he just happened to enjoy collecting old maps. I suppose one could consider it to be a hobby of his! Perhaps someone gave it to him whilst he was abroad. To tell you the truth I have no idea how he acquired it. But is this significant?"

"It could be at that. Monte Cara, Mindelo's deepwater port is connected to the bay which is itself an extinct underwater volcanic crater. That coupled with the chart markings of the Cape Verde Abyss could prove to be very significant indeed!"

By this time she must have been listening with her lips slightly ajar for Gregg nudged her to bring her back to reality and with that she hastened to question the speaker further.

"So suppose you are right in this. Does it really make any difference to anyone outside of your immediate club?"

"Finding the suspected location of such a place that is prime for investigation could be worth a considerable amount of money. So tell me please, how much do you want for the map Miss Craven?"

"It is not for sale. You people don't get it do you? This map is one of the last things I possess that once belonged to my father, a man I now believe I should have strived to have known better in his lifetime!"

Surprisingly enough Helmut seemed to be rather pleased with her response " I think that perhaps your father did have good foundations for his theory!" He spoke at length. "Glancing generally at the positioning of these Islands it is within the realms of possibility that the site of the lost city could be in their midst. You don't mind if I check up on something do you?" He had already opened up his computer even before she nodded her head in agreement. A few dabs later and a look of extreme interest flooded his face.

"From what I have just gleaned it is said that many, many years ago a meteorite struck the Earth in this region. That could account for the almost symmetrical circle of the Islands here around this sea. There is no doubt that such an intense collision would have triggered off some rather violent activity within the area to a far larger scale than what is believed to have happened around Santorini!" He glanced at Gregg with a smile. "It appears my friend that we could have been searching all this time in the wrong places for it is far more likely that the site we have been searching for is in this area!"

"So even if you believe that there is some possible truth in this new evidence what do you propose we should do about it? Surely the sea in these parts is far too deep to even contemplate a dive?"

"Well certainly not in the centre of the chasm I agree with you on that. But then there is nothing to stop us from taking one of the local boats out and try to test the water for certain impurities within it. Indeed such an action could prove to be highly significant and help us a great deal in producing a paper on the matter!"

"Sorry but this time I did promise Josie that I would go on a trip with her around the Island!" Gregg glanced at her meaningfully almost daring her to defy him. In the meantime Helmut looked at his friend a trifle despondently.

"I didn't assume we had come on this mission to socialise but if you must I suppose I could always ask Paul if he would give me a hand!"

Gregg noticed Josie stiffen at his words but it was Helmut who followed his eyes. "Paul Butler did not kill your father Josie. In fact if the truth is known he was the one who climbed down the precipice in a futile effort to save the man's life!"

"I ought to ask how you know about my business but instead I will merely pose the question that if Paul Butler did not kill my father who exactly did push him over that crevice?"

"Have you thought of asking Paul Butler that yourself? The man had his suspicions but at the time had little to base his theory on. But quite recently things appear to have become a great deal clearer. I believe we took a new passenger on board at La Gomera!"

"You are speaking of Baron Aldermatt I presume. Well much as I deplore the man it appears, at least according to what he has already told me, that he was a good acquaintance of my father. Therefore if his words are to be believed why on earth would the man want to kill him and why did I see Paul Butler approaching him with a weapon earlier on today?"

"The first part of your question is probably the easier to answer. Maybe your father felt able to relax in the Baron's company and perhaps therefore he actually told him something of his own special interest in the collection of these maps. As for the answer to the second part of your question I suggest you ask Paul Butler to answer that for himself."

Helmut nodded over her shoulder and Josie turned to follow his gaze for she hadn't realised that the man they had been speaking about had now come into the library and was standing behind them. Nor in point of fact did this person appear too pleased to be included in her company for the man in question suddenly spun round. "If we have to join forces, Miss Craven, which is something of which I still disapprove, then don't you think it is time you made a gesture and handed over that weapon you are carrying?" The eyes that she met were startlingly blue without any hint of friendship extended within them. "Quite frankly woman you give me the creeps simply carrying it around on your person. For starters I don't expect that you have a clue at how to use it plus the fact I can hardly see C allowing a novice to handle live bullets!"

"If you must know I carry it because I believe that your boss has got every confidence in me!" She was determined that she was not going to yield one inch.

"Well one supposes that C always did have a soft spot as far as women are concerned; plus the fact it is often said that sometimes it proves necessary to tell a small falsehood if only to shut a woman up!"

"Hi there steady on mate, perhaps that is a little bit close to the knuckle even considering the remark came from you!" At least Gregg appeared to have taken in her current expression and was now offering her some support.

"Oh yes! And there was I believing you when you said that trying to make love to a woman wearing that sort of equipment was going to prove damned difficult!"

"What exactly did you mean when you mentioned joining forces?" She ignored his comments and instead faced Paul Butler still not quite sure what had brought on this change of heart. "I don't think I mentioned the prospect of joining forces with you. Indeed nothing could be further from my mind at this moment in time, especially after what I have recently learnt about your exploits on the upper deck!"

"You may have opted out of the course at University but even so the fact that two people disembarked at La Gomera and were replaced cannot have escaped your attention if you were concentrating with even the partial intelligence that initially secured you a place on the University course!"

"I was aware that you were one of their replacements at La Gomera yes and I was also aware that you made an attempt on the other passenger's life!" She nodded as she spat out her gleaned information whilst ignoring his reference to her failure on the law degree. After all Paul Butler was so single minded that any emotions she might have had appeared to count for little.

"And in truth you were the one who put paid to me completing an assignment Miss Craven!" She was still convinced the man showed hatred in his eyes.

"Perhaps if you two stop bickering we could get back to the reason for this meeting!" Helmut by this time appeared frustrated. "I believe that if you take a closer look at this map which Miss Craven has provided you will agree that there are now more important issues than listening to the pair of you going at it hammer and tongues!"

At least glancing in the direction of the map appeared to abate a little of Paul Butler's anger. "So having become convinced that this is the site you were searching for what is next on the agenda?"

"I was hoping that you would take a local boat trip with me tomorrow so that we could take some water samples!"

Butler looked questioningly at Gregg. "And what of your friend here?"

"I understand he has made a promise to Miss Craven to explore the Island with her!"

"Sorry, but no can do!" He still regarded her with some insolence. "Whilst I agree it is something of a sad thing to interrupt the passage of a lover's tryst I am afraid that I happen to have a business appointment on the Island and therefore your colleague will have to show some willingness to forgo some of the pleasure he appears to have mapped out for himself. Sorry Gregg but my appointment is of prime importance and therefore your affairs of the heart will have to take a back seat!"

To her surprise Gregg nodded in agreement. In truth she had never expected this man to be side tracked into this situation and leaving the map where it was on the table for to have gathered it up would have proved an embarrassment to her, she turned and left the library before anyone could call her back!

On deck early the following morning Josie however had to admit that all she had previously read about an African sunrise was a sheer understatement; for the vivid redness of the sky silhouetting the mountain peaks of the African continent before such a herald gave way with one last triumphant fanfare as the ball of sunlight appeared clearly on the horizon and which consequently moved to ride the heavens in its majestic splendour, was something reminiscent of an ancient world that was trying to come to terms with a modern conception. This whole episode did not take very long in minutes on man's time clock but nevertheless it was enough to leave an indelible impression upon her memory. Meanwhile the ship that was obviously uninspired by this spectacle ploughed steadily on through quieter waters whilst even the waters of the on deck swimming pool now appeared to obey these new strictures of the natural world and kept steadily within the confines of their allotted aperture.

Standing there watching as the reflection of the quickly risen sun formed a pathway to eternity across those waters Josie wasn't at first aware that she had been joined on the deck by Gregg, his face still bearing the scars of retribution for the way that they had parted the previous evening.

"Look I guess I'm sorry for what happened yesterday if that is any consolation!" Now she could almost imagine a naughty schoolboy glancing down at his feet as he twisted the soles of his shoes from side to side.

"I believe breakfast is being served outside this morning by the pool!" Josie didn't know whether she had uttered these words in an attempt to reassure him or whether she was simply stating an established fact in order to find at least something to say to him. She glanced past the pool where by this time some early bathers were already immersed in those waters to take in the trail that the boat left behind on its journey south without realising that his eyes were now taking in her sun apparel with a look of approval.

"Then perhaps we ought to consider joining the rest to partake in it!" He nodded in the direction of the lower deck where the tables had already been graced with tablecloths along with parasols to shield those sitting there from the sun's fiercest rays. She smiled her assent for she supposed that to be able to eat with Gregg in such a setting and without the others in attendance was a bonus, even if the prospect of them being alone still caused a feeling of timidity to beset her. Yet now she was determined not to allow her emotions enter into the matter.

"Helmut is still going on about that map you provided us with!" He volunteered the statement as they moved to rescue their croissants from the poolside bar. "Tomorrow promises to be a very exciting day for him!"

The words stung her taking her back to what had transpired the previous evening when Gregg had in a way broken a promise to her. "And I would say an exciting day for yourself too!" Her words were clipped although she still wondered why he had placed the onus on Helmut.

"Me, you know jolly well that I would have preferred to have spent the day touring the Island with you!"

"Well I managed to book an excursion after I left you last night. You see it appeared to be a great pity to have come all this way and not to see what the place has to offer. Besides I understood you were here to dive or take a boat out or whatever, especially as now it appears that your colleague Paul Butler is unable to stay with Helmut so I really cannot understand your reason for apologising!" At least she determined that she would emerge from this conversation without loss of face!

"Let's say I did believe that there was a time and a place for everything and in truth I did at the time also believe that he would have his colleague to accompany him even if I did happen to be wrong in my thinking!" Perhaps now Gregg was attempting to justify what had transpired but Josie was hard to convince.

"I suppose you are now referring to Paul Butler?" Her face changed at the very mention of the man's name.

"Why not try and forget about the man Josie. I don't really suppose you will ever find it in your heart to like him, but in truth he did not kill your father. That is something that I think even you are already beginning to accept considering that I note you have managed to part yourself from that hideous toy you have been carrying around!"

His eyes must have searched her form although in truth she had decided that there was literally no way she could have concealed it, not in the flimsy attire she was currently wearing.

"How can I possibly forget him? I was employed to seek the man out!" She deliberately ignored Gregg's reference to the weapon.

"I cannot expect that even your organisation, as dim witted as what they can sometimes appear to be to seriously expect to employ you simply to kill one man to order. In fact I will go as far as to say that I believe Josie Craven that you were taken for one big fall guy in this even if it was only initiated in the first place in order to shut you up. In fact I wouldn't be at all surprised if you were to find your so-called ammunition faulty. In fact possibly the whole scenario would have made a far better plot for your namesake Kimberley Clark than what it does for you!"

She felt her face flushing a burning red, which contrasted with the sea mist that had now completely obscured the African coast but had at least tempered some of the entire force of sun's rays from beating down on them. "Still you asked about Helmut, what about your own new found girl companion?"

"You mean Fern. I haven't actually set eyes on her this morning!"

"She is a strange person is that one. I suppose one could consider that it was also strange in the way she first found you!"

Josie was silent. Now she pondered on that phone call the girl had been making and the way the other had behaved at the time: At the time it had almost appeared as if she held a secret that she refused to have prised out of her. "Anyway presuming that you have forgiven me for backtracking on that excursion we planned to take together, what are your thoughts for today?"

Josie stretched out her legs and wriggled her toes so that they fit more comfortably in her sandals. In truth she had failed to consider anything past having breakfast in the relative peace and quiet of the early morning. "In truth I confess that I have not given the day too much thought apart from basking in a little of the sunshine especially after what we left behind at home!"

"A little sunshine must be the operative word. Remember our present latitude for I believe we have now crossed the Tropic of Cancer, at least if the sudden alteration in our watches is anything to go by, all of which makes it a dangerous location for sampling the sun. Still I do suggest that we could possibly partake in a swim. This could be followed if you like by deck shuffleboard on the starboard side that is out of the direct sunlight this morning. I did consider the gym but then decided that such an activity would be far too energy sapping in this sort of weather!"

"I'll take you up on the swim anyway!" For the life of her she couldn't say why she suddenly agreed for spending time with him in any activity had been the last thing on her mind.

"Do you wish to remain here or shall we try the one on the upper deck? I suppose it all depends on how deep you appreciate your water, the one on the upper deck being slightly shallower!" If he had sensed any reticence on her part then he deliberately ignored it.

"As I consider that I have been watching this pool slop over the sides in rough weather perhaps I am tempted to say that we could sample what this place has to offer!"

"A swim not followed by a Jacuzzi but rather a coffee!" He had just spotted Helmut heading towards those round tubs that contained warm water that sent up pillars of steam in cooler climes. It was yet another tangled mystery to Josie as to why the man she was currently with now wished to avoid the person he was supposed to be travelling with.

Still the lifts appeared to be working to full capacity by this time and so Josie decided to take the stairs in order to collect her gear: She was in fact just in the process of passing the point that led to the Main deck when she spotted Fern close by the Reception area. At the time the girl appeared to be intent in conversation and therefore she obviously did not notice Josie, but it was the person to whom Fern was talking that made Josie blink her eyes in surprise. She looked again but there could be no mistake for alongside of the display of photographs that had already been taken of the voyage Fern appeared to be deep in conversation with Paul Butler!

Waking up to that scene of the port of Mindelo on the Island of Sao Vincente surrounded by lofty mountainous peaks was something that she deemed could only truly have happened in a dream and she almost automatically pinched herself to see if she was really awake. So this was the Caldera, the crater that had been left by underwater volcanic activity in the era of pre history and which made the splendour of Santorini almost appear miniscule in comparison.

Once they had berthed they found themselves surrounded by the brightly coloured ships of the local traders in this former Portuguese colony and alongside those a coastguard boat whose members were currently ashore enjoying a well deserved haircut. But the day was a Sunday, a day that was strictly observed by the smiling population who still carried their wares in a traditional African fashion even though there were still many traces of its colonial heritage. Yet this factor was not really observed in the clamour of folk anxious to get off the boat and see things for themselves.

The coaches left the port at eleven o'clock, eleven of them altogether, so that they could feast their eyes upon the sights that once the wealthy English had accepted as a way of life when they had perambulated in the shade of the Praca Nova in white apparel, listening at the same time to the strains put out by the local musicians for there was little doubt that music still played a large part in the lives of the locals and Josie remembered the local brass band that had turned out to greet their arrival earlier on at the port. The square had been a place where long ago only the English had been privileged to walk but now it was accustomed to the tread of many nationalities

Yet away from the town with its wide esplanades around the harbour the journey up into that mountainous region of the Pik D'Zau was something that would not have been considered amiss in the space age and despite what one might have expected from the latitude it was a place covered in greenery with ample evidence of folk busy gathering in their crops. A journey that Josie decided was well worth the indignity of travelling along the cobble stone roads in the antiquated motorised transport that had been placed at their disposal.

Even so she was still glad when the breeze decided to rouse itself at lunchtime to temper the hot sun. It had been present when she had been up on the mountain, enjoying the view over the town and its port but once back again in the town it had grown stiflingly hot. Finally moving yet again she was to spot Helmut and Gregg now fully occupied around the beach area of Cat Fish Bay and by this time Helmut appeared to be besides himself in excitement, for now knowledge of the map she had supplied and the fact that the boat had berthed in the Baia de Porto Grande had spurred him on to believe that this truly must be the place to seek evidence of that lost city.

For her own part however Josie preferred to ignore them and to concentrate instead upon the musical extravaganza that the locals had put on to impress their guests in a ranch type dwelling not too far from the shore. Yet she was more than a little surprised when amongst the countless number of visitors who were there at the time she was to spot the likeness of Fern alongside of Paul Butler. For Paul to be there rather than attending to a business appointment was the bigger surprise for to her mind Fern could easily explain her own presence at that gathering even if this had been to attempt to gather inspiration for one of her paintings. Unless, she reminded herself, Paul's business appointment had encircled Fern in the first place for she remembered seeing them talking in that Reception area back on the boat.

Yet a further surprise was to wipe all thoughts of seeing them here temporarily from her mind for with all the coaches now present it came as a shock to her to now spot Baron Aldermatt. Surely such a tourist attraction was not something that one would have expected this man to want to participate in? In addition she had believed that this same Baron was due to leave the ship once it had berthed here.

Perhaps the person in question read her thoughts when he spotted her for he hastened to cross the hacienda to join her.

"You are enjoying Mindelo Miss Craven?" The man struggled to afford her a greasy smile and flash his ageing teeth at her. Josie quickly decided that if it was so much of a struggle for him to do this she would have been far more relieved if he had not bothered.

"Yes, very much. I guess it is quite an experience to find a green oasis such as this so far south!" She steeled herself to make her reply quickly instructing herself that it was far better for this man not to witness any turbulence of thought on her part.

"Of course I wholeheartedly agree with you and what is more it is a place that is ripe for development. I can almost see the advertisements for it ----A Pirates Island well into the Atlantic!"

"So is that the reason why you are here?" She had seen the signs of new constructions being erected and in fact the guide on the bus had reluctantly admitted that there was such development but not yet enough of the commercialism that the people needed.

"I consider that is a good enough reason. Such phases as the Islands once being a penal colony and a place that was once embroiled in the slave trade are possibly factors that will hold out some appeal to our Northern culture. After all one must always have an eye towards the end of the current recession because when it is finally established people will want to seek out new places to visit for their pleasure. In fact if you were to take a look in the Marina close to where the boat docked you will already see quite a number of large yachts moored there. That I believe is a sign of things to come, therefore who can blame me if I seek to invest now whilst the price is still favourable?"

"So you will be staying on here then?" Her eyes focussed on the place where the white sand met the clean blue waters whilst behind her at the time the local traditional folk music surrounded the Mindelo Carnival Kings and Queens.

"No I have a business deal to conclude in Praia, the capital of these Islands when the boat docks there tomorrow and the Captain has assured me that there will be no difficulty in accommodating me for an extra night. In the meantime however I intend to make the most of my day here. I believe your friends are already busy with their self-appointed task and therefore I will be very interested to hear of their conclusions!" He bowed in a manner to excuse himself that Josie found almost ridiculous. Indeed she would have found the whole episode amusing had she not already suspected something of the darker side of this man's character. She watched as he deliberately made his way over towards where Fern and Paul were now standing watching the dancing that resembled more of a tribal greeting, yet much to her surprise it was not Paul whom the Baron made to speak to but Fern whilst Paul himself looked somewhat put out at the situation

Eventually as she returned to the ship she spotted Helmut and Gregg who were also returning after spending the regulatory time under the water. She had been a little surprised at this remembering what Gregg had previously said about just taking water samples but realised that the fact that Helmut had decided to dive after all in the shallower waters of that Bay was a possible explanation as to why Gregg had changed his mind to go with his friend after all, particularly as the other one had not been available and it required two divers to enter the water together. Moreover they appeared to have hired a three-wheeled moped to make the journey from the port along the twisting mountainous track that was more than often covered only with a pebbled surface and resembled something of a lunar landscape. Moreover there seemed also to be a variety of different ways of crossing that Island, for whilst Josie had ventured out by the formal coach, that could hardly be said to be of European standards they had passed hikers, jeeps and even the captain of the ship who was at the time gaining his daily exercise by cycling. Now she noted that Helmut in particular was looking particularly pleased with himself and they had also appeared to deliberately ignore any of the local festivities that had been organised for the guests. Still it was Gregg who upon meeting her who was the one eager to tell their story.

"I guess Helmut thinks that the whole scenario appears to be very promising. In fact that map which belonged to your father was obviously spot on. Of course we still have other places that we need to explore before we can reach a firm conclusion but at this moment in time all I can say is that it seems to be highly significant in what we have located. One has to admit however that one current strand of thought is that the ancient city still lies around where Santorini presently stands, but in all truth this place appears to offer much more than that!"

"But surely the very depth of the ocean around these shores makes it literally impossible for anyone to be sure about it, doesn't it?" She remembered seeing the Abyss chasm of Cape Verde out in the sea not far from the shores of these Islands and by this time Gregg appeared to have forgotten all about his previous arrangement with her in his general furore of excitement.

"At the moment you are probably quite right in what you say but at least the location of this place will provide fuel in the scripting of the paper that Helmut has to produce for I believe that this place is just as valid as any other you would care to mention. In fact Helmut is still bemoaning the fact that he spent so much of his time promoting the fact that the lost city must lie somewhere off the Canary islands instead of so far south. But these Islands were on the old established trade routes and well utilised possibly even before modern civilisation, as we know it, was established. And yet I still owe you an apology for letting you down today therefore I promise that if you will forgive me then I will make it up to you!"

She supposed the man looked so beguiling that she nodded her agreement and then immediately chastised herself for doing so. After all she was not supposed to be here to socialise and the memory of seeing Fern together with Paul Butler again flooded her thoughts and troubled her mind!

Such thoughts on Fern Astor were perhaps a precursor of things yet to come for she was to meet the woman on the way to her cabin to get changed before the evening meal. Whether or not this meeting was purely accidental or by design as Josie strongly suspected it was, remained however a matter for conjecture for the woman appeared to now have reverted into her charming most beguiling self.

"Did you have a good day then?" Obviously the woman had far more than Josie's appreciation on her mind for even as she spoke she was wafting her art file in the air to make sure that Josie noticed it. "Guess I've been finishing off my sketches from Mindelo!"

So that was the obvious crunch line, the woman wanted Josie's appreciation. From her own point of view perhaps Josie with her underlying caring nature decided that Fern had remained in the cold for far too long and therefore even if she did not initial feel this way she attempted to at least feign some interest in the contents of the folder that Fern obviously now wanted to show her. Therefore she raised no objection when Fern followed her back to her cabin for at least in that place, as opposed to opening her file in the companionway, the girl would have at least a little space to show the contents of her work.

In fact upon viewing these sketches Josie began to show some appreciation of the girl's work for Fern had decidedly captured some of the ethos of that Castaway Island. But maybe what intrigued Josie more was a photograph that fell out from amongst these sketches. At first Fern appeared anxious to rescue the same claiming that taking photographs of any subject matter usually helped her at a later stage to finalise her artwork.

This explanation seemed to be fair enough until Josie actually saw the contents of that photograph for the subject matter appeared to be of two people talking together, herself and Baron Aldermatt when they had met in the grounds of the hacienda.

"I was surprised when I noticed that you knew our additional passenger!" The girl was obviously trying to cover up some of the dismay she felt at Josie actually seeing the photograph.

"We had met on a previous occasion yes!" Josie felt herself tensing for in truth she was now beginning to wonder what the girl was getting at besides puzzling her reasons for wanting to take this shot in the first place. "In actual fact I was as surprised as what you apparently were upon seeing him on the ship, but after meeting him again when we were on the Island it seemed to be only polite to exchange the time of day. Still perhaps I am even more surprised by the fact that you found it necessary to take a photograph of us for after all I hardly consider that we made useful topics for your art work!"

"Sorry if I offended you but in actual fact the photograph was not aimed at you but rather at the whole of the gathering, but the two of you just happened to be in the frame at the time so that is why your images are now on film!"

Josie wondered whether the girl was actually floundering to find excuses or whether she was right and the taking of this shot had been a mere accident. The fact that she had no way of telling bugged her even more. Still now having imparted what she had initially intended the girl appeared anxious to leave her.

"Guess I'm stopping you from getting ready, I had better go!" Josie nodded and made no attempt to stop her as she made for the door for now she was left to puzzle out for herself whether indeed Fern had wanted in the first place to show her the sketches or whether indeed it had been the means to disguise the photograph. Moreover if the latter happened to be the truth and the photograph had been dropped deliberately then why had she done this, or had she been advised to do so by another person and could that other person be the one whom she appeared to have spent the day with, Paul Butler?

★ ★ ★ ★

Chapter Seven

She supposed Gregg had chosen the time to put forward the idea when they were dancing that evening during the hosted session that was significantly timed to take place between the two evening shows in the Neptune Lounge. At the time the trumpet coupled with the trombone were playing what amounted to a seductive mellow sound in their music. Clothed now in garlands to mark the tropical evening on board Josie had already sensed her heart beating almost in tandem with the drums as the two of them moved even closer on that dance floor and she quickly realised that Gregg had felt something of this mood too for he was certainly reluctant to release his hold when the dance had finally reached a conclusion.

"Tomorrow I swear I will make it up to you. I have already taken the liberty of hiring some wheels when we berth in Praia. Helmut if you must know is by this time completely absorbed in the compilation of his findings so far and I think my wheels will prove infinitely better than travelling in one of those coaches in order to see something of the Island. Therefore I am asking you if you will consider coming with me?"

"You mean that tomorrow you have no intention of diving?"

"That I can fervently promise you! In any case Helmut appears to be completely satisfied in what we have achieved so far. Therefore can I take it that you have forgiven me for today and you will come with me, always providing of course that you can trust in my company for half a day spent sight seeing?"

Could she trust him? That indeed was a laugh especially after considering the way she felt about him! "But how will you know what there is to see in Praia? I take it that you have not been there before? I presumed it was a first for both of us."

"Well if you must know I have managed to cajole my way into getting a very good guide book to the place!" He tapped the pocket of his jacket meaningfully. "Plus the fact I have every intention of swotting up all the salient facts in bed tonight. Can I take it that your answer is yes Miss Craven?"

Josie nodded her head. In all truth travelling in those coaches that were adequate but still left quite a lot to be desired didn't totally appeal to her after her first experience. Besides her heart had shouted out to make itself heard that to be able to be on her own with this man, and therefore even if the duration was destined to be but one half day, it nevertheless held great promise. In fact she was so taken with the idea that any thought of

Fern and that photograph that she may initially have held faded from her memory

"Good, then I guess that is settled!" He bent over and kissed her nose his arms lingering longer than was absolutely necessary on her shoulders but then it appeared they were to be joined by the others and so propriety became the order of the day!

What however Josie didn't know was that long after she retired that night Gregg spent a frantic hour phoning around in order to secure a car for hire and then he was to spend the rest of the night swotting up on the local knowledge that he had been offered!

Praira de Santa Maria, which served as the capital city for the whole of the archipelago and was the main port on the Island of Santiago, which was the largest of the Cape Verde Islands seemed to be just as awe inspiring to behold as its more northerly cousin as the ship sailed through the red of the morning sun into its volcanic mass. Yet even if this place that sat on a small plateaus above the natural harbour depicted the fact that this was where time stood still, the early morning activity around the pool area on the boat decried this. Indeed the Volcan giants of the ancients, who possibly still stood sentinel over their creation must have indeed laughed at beholding man's present day endeavours; man who firmly believed that he alone was both the conqueror and explorer of the earth. Yet now these ancients remained silent like the Greek gods of old who had watched man's struggle in the Odyssey; aye, and taken the opportunity to challenge him on every move he had made!

Slowly, very slowly, the curtain of mist that protected this Island rose from off its peaks to expose the undulating and unforgiving landscape as the ship drew closer. The passengers on that vessel were destined only for a short stay here but already the elements were busy exacting a captivating charm enough to capture and imprison man's soul!

Despite his determination to spend the time here with Josie, Gregg nevertheless had still felt a sense of relief when Helmut had declared that diving at this place was not on the agenda and that he had certainly not changed his mind for there were certain facts that he wished instead to calibrate in the museum there. It was a matter that he had made quite clear to Gregg when they had passed by Fire Island the previous evening and Helmut had spotted the sight of the volcano that was still active on the Island of Fogo where no one was now allowed to land and from where all the previous residents had been evacuated in fear for their lives. Perhaps this indeed had been the one factor that had been enough to finally determine him that the chasm of this ocean was the place he had sought after for so long in order to solve its mystery.

Therefore the quick phone call that he had made had been sufficient enough to hire Gregg the benefit of that waiting jeep and the latter felt he could now afford to acquiesce knowing that at least Josie would be spared the discomfort of those local coaches along the undulating cobbled roads!

The drive of course gave Gregg the opportunity to surprise her with the local knowledge he had studied during the previous night and he was therefore aptly able to point out to her such things as the Island that lay just off the shore, which had once housed the lepers of that colony and was still referred to by that name.

"Not only that but there has certainly been one recent suggestion that the Island could now house a Casino!"

"Surely not!" She suddenly felt aghast at the idea of such a commercial enterprise in a place where once people had suffered so abysmally.

"No, I guess I took the opportunity of speaking to one of the guides whilst I was waiting for you and apparently the locals were up in arms against the idea and consequently the thought died a lingering death. Not that there isn't plenty of poverty still around for apparently twenty per cent of the populace still live in one room without adequate sanitation although apparently they all have a television set!"

Josie let out a laugh at her companion's determination to relate his findings. "Do you know something Josie, laughter suits you! In fact I consider you really should try to laugh more often!"

She suddenly sobered. "How did these people first come to inhabit these Islands, did you manage to find that out as well?"

"Basically I suppose you can say that the indigenous population came by way of the slave trade. We are heading away now from the main tourist area towards the green valley that first gave the place its name when they arrived here from Senegal. In fact Cidade Velna is perhaps the oldest settlement in the Cape Verde Islands.

Nevertheless even before that time these Islands were always a sort of stopping off place on the trade routes. But then fortunately or otherwise many of those who were destined to be sold at the slave market managed to escape up into the mountains, hence the current indigenous black population we have today along with their Creole language, which was the primitive form of communication they first developed although in truth many European languages are taught here as well as used, including our own. Anyway the locals here still maintain that the scourge of their past happens to be Sir Francis Drake whom they still regard as being a pirate because he removed all the riches from the Island to present to Good Queen Bess back home and consequently the French pirates who were to follow, finding nothing left that was of any value to them then set fire to the place although in retrospect our own national hero did attempt to make amends when he gave the Islanders six canons that you can still see mounted around the fort today!"

"So presumably if the maps that my father left bears some significance and Helmut does manage to publish the paper he is on about then it is highly likely that the place will begin to prosper again this time with tourists?"

"Maybe you have hit the nail on the head with that assumption. Not that the tourists don't manage to stray here already for we are living proof of that by being here ourselves, but I suppose they will come in far larger numbers if that paper is published!"

It being a Monday the Municipal Market was going in full swing and Josie was fascinated with the throb of activity, with the baskets of exotic fish lying there on the ground, with the women carrying their heavy loads upon their heads and especially with the girl tour guide who had obviously broken the strap on her sandal but was still determined to conduct her business in that place wearing only one shoe. Later they were to wander through the settlement of Cidade Velha the oldest settlement on the Island with its stone buildings in the shadow of the fifteenth century fortress and onto the old slave quarters where the locals still utilised the old scrubbing boards to do the weekly wash usually watched keenly by the rest of the family and onto the fort that had once been attacked by Francis Drake and finally into the square that at one time had served as the official slave market, where once the slaves had been priced but which now was used by the locals to ply their wares in a market style fashion. They watched as one of the local women carried a heavy basket of fruit on her head leaving the older residents to sit in the shade playing the same tympani of sound on crafted drums in the same way as they had played once upon a time to alleviate some of the suffering that these slaves chained to a pole had once endured. From there the two passed onto the beach of fine sand washed by the tide that had allowed it to keep its sandy colouration.

Allowing those waves to trickle through her toes Josie felt Gregg's arm again around her shoulders and began to realise that the previous night had been no dream. It was a time now to forget the others and what her task entailed and concentrate instead on her own emotions. Now she no longer felt that she cared about the true purpose that lay behind this voyage and instead wished with all her heart that these moments spent alone with Gregg would never come to an end.

Yet the whole episode was destined to come to an end sooner than what she thought for even as he drew her close as they waited their turn to re board the ship it became evident that Helmut was waiting there for them wearing a rather doleful expression.

"It's that woman, the one whom you brought to share our table!" His eyes stared almost accusingly in Josie's direction.

"Fern do you mean?" In truth Josie had seen little of the girl not since she had apparently rekindled some sort of friendship with Paul Butler although the memory of the occasion in her cabin the previous afternoon did finally jog at her thoughts.

"Yes, the bitch tried to get her hands on some of my findings!" The irritation in the Dutchman's voice was obvious. "I was under the impression that the woman was interested in paintings not scientific findings! I was working in the library at the time and had left my dissertation on the table because the ship appeared to be quiet, everyone having gone ashore. I guess it's a good job that Paul happened to catch her in the act. What I would like to know is who exactly is that woman and more importantly who the hell is she working for? There's something else as well she made a great deal of fuss of that other intruder when he left the ship!"

"The other intruder?"

"Yes the one who cadged a lift. The Baron or whatever you call him?"

"So I take it that Baron Aldermatt has finally departed?" At least she wasn't sorry to see the back of that intimidating creature even if her face had now flushed up at the thought of the previous day.

"With a bit of luck he has. There was something about that guy that I can't really say that I cared for!"

So she was not the only one to share such sentiments. Even so Josie mentioned nothing about the incident although quite frankly she felt quite relieved that the man had finally left the ship.

"So what of yourself?" Helmut now looked questioning at Josie as if he had suddenly remembered her own initial quest.

"The lady is with me!" Gregg sounded determined to his colleague but at the same time he smiled a note of confidence in Josie's direction.

"If that is the case then what do you think your bosses will have to say about that?" The Dutchman was still persistent. "Forgive me but I believe I have had enough upsets on this endeavour with the other one you conveniently managed to pick up. I'm only glad that Paul happened to be around to stop her before all our findings disappeared, although who would want to buy them at this stage is a different matter!"

"But I thought that Paul and Fern appeared to get on well together?" At least she brought herself to query that relationship.

"Who Paul Butler and this Fern character, you must be joking!" For his part Helmut appeared incensed and it was now left to Gregg to defuse the situation.

"I don't think you need to worry about Josie. In the first place she was issued with a gun that could not have fired at anyone anyway!"

Helmut turned upon her again his eyes wide open. "But who on earth would have wanted to have done a thing like that? I'm afraid that your British Intelligence leaves me feeling very confused."

"In that you are not on your own!" Josie decided that the time had possibly come for her to speak up for herself. "Who knows perhaps the powers that be simply wanted to get rid of me and shut up my bleating down their ears, although why on earth they cited Paul Butler as being the principle transgressor in all of this is quite beyond me!"?

"I believe someone mentioned my name?" The man in the conversation appeared now to have returned to the fold.

"Yes Paul. Tell me, why exactly you are on this boat if you can? After all you were not on it when we first set sail!" For in truth if their masks were about to be finally discarded then Josie determined that she would get her facts right. Paul however returned her rhetoric with a look of surprise that she should have so questioned him.

"I wonder why it is that you were never quite so observant when we started University. All you appeared to want to do at that time was to be able to opt out and play at being Vivien Leigh somewhere? But if it is necessary for you to know I am here because I was told that it was most essential for me to be present, whether that was in order to give you the opportunity to shoot me or not remains something that I do not know. No, please don't look like that for the actual reasons that were given to me remain a secret. Still after complying with the orders given to me I was rather fortunate to find two of my old friends on board, more especially as I happen to share Helmut's enthusiasm as a hobby and I was glad to be able to be of some service to him today! So what is your next question Madame Detective?" There seemed to be little doubt that the man was more than a little annoyed at her impertinence in questioning some of his actions and Josie swallowed hard.

"Why not leave the girl alone Paul. As far as I can see Josie only wanted to know about your own role in all of this for after all she has now found herself to be on something like a fool's errand so it is only natural that she wants to ask questions!" It was Gregg who had interceded yet again, much to the surprise of the other two.

"Then perhaps she ought to go and seek her answers from those who sent her!"

"So what have you done with Fern this afternoon?" This time it was Helmut who posed the question still bearing a frown on his face

"I guess I haven't seen anything of the girl since I disturbed her in the library and she went ashore. She must be back now though although she seemed to have somewhere in mind when she first left the ship and I can assure you that it wasn't to catch one of those coaches and that includes the shuttle service into the town!"

"Perhaps it was to gather inspiration for her art work. I know that she has attended some of the sessions here on board!"

Josie considered she was being helpful but by this time Paul had obviously had enough of this conversation for he made to drift away from them. It was then that Gregg finally turned to Josie.

"So what have you in mind for this afternoon after we have grabbed a spot of lunch?"

For her part Josie tried to focus her mind back onto the ship's activities scheduled for that day but found that at that time her mind seemed to draw a blank. "Perhaps a dip in the pool followed by a spot of relaxation!"

Helmut scoffed laudably at her words. "Well I for one will be returning to the library in an attempt to finish off my report so that I will be able to fax the details back when we get to Tenerife. After all I consider that all this relaxation is good for no sane person!"

"In that case you will have to excuse me Helmut because I think that I will try a little of Josie's method of relaxation for all work is of no use to any man, that is always providing she will have me tagging along with her of course!"

Josie's heart sang for it sounded as if the brief interlude that the two of them had shared whilst in Praira was not yet over and for once, much to her surprise, Helmut appeared to raise no objections!

On deck they were now serving a lunch of paella whilst the drinks flowed freely, the chefs accomplished their ice carvings and the band played for their entertainment and it felt good to have Gregg to herself for a time even if she still questioned her feelings about the man for these where emotions that she never ever dreamed that she would find and she still wondered if she was encapsulated in a dream from which she must surely awake!

Fern did not make another appearance until it was time for the evening meal. At the time Josie and Gregg were sharing a drink together in the lounge bar and Josie was marvelling at how the relationship between them was developing when the girl appeared, looking completely ravishing in an emerald green evening dress; a factor that surprised Josie for she had not credited Fern with being the sort of person who desired to dress formally for any occasion.

"Have you had a good day?" At least she supposed that she had to say something although in response to this question the other girl wrinkled her nose in a rather distasteful manner.

"Others may be tempted to call it that, but I myself beg to differ. As far as I was concerned merely spotting those women carrying heavy baskets containing almost everything seemed to have evolved from some bygone era was quite enough to put anyone off!"

"Well it is Africa after all and their mode of life is quite different to our own. But what of the inspiration for your art work?"

"I'm afraid I found nothing inspiring in that seedbed of humanity!"

"Still if you had wanted to escape the hustle and bustle of market life perhaps you should have caught one of those coaches that were going farther a field!"

"I missed the deadline for booking on one of those trips unfortunately but to make up for it I pampered myself in the spa when I returned from trudging those streets in the hot sun!" She sported her new hair do that unfortunately did little to enhance her features for it made her look a rather hard and manipulative woman.

It was Helmut who appeared to cast the final disapproving glance in the girl's direction. "The question is do you consider it was worth the money?"

"Take no notice of him!" The girl had gasped and Gregg now tried to whisper almost encouragingly to her. "After all it can be said that Helmut disapproves of anything that happens to fall outside of his subject matter!" Then turning to the other man. "By the way, I saw you round the office, did you manage to complete your report and fax it off after all?"

"Had the devil of a job with the satellite I admit but yes, I took a chance bearing in mind that others appear a little too eager to interfere with my findings, a goodly portion of the whole now being completed!" Again he glared in Fern's direction.

"Of course you would have to misinterpret my intentions. I was actually looking for some of my own work that I had left there previously!" And after stating her case Fern made to move away from them

Even so Helmut still snorted in disbelief at her words and would possibly have called after her if Gregg once again had not hastened to defuse the situation

"In that case Helmut if you have finally managed to send your thesis off perhaps you will now find a little more time to relax!"

"Hardly for I consider the whole to be far from completed. I still need to consider the effect of the Mid Atlantic Ridge on the matter!"

Josie must have looked puzzled for Helmut regarded her rather disdainfully. "Yes I am referring now to the centre of the earthquake and consequent volcanic activity of course!" He spoke like a learned professor to some inane student and perhaps for the first time Josie began to realise just how knowledgeable this man really was.

Still it was Gregg who decided that it was time to share more of her company and therefore stepped onto the scene to entice her away for personally he now wanted no interference in the new relationship with Josie that he had formed. Josie for her part however still cast a glance at the by now disappearing Fern for there was definitely now something about this girl that she had once found friendly that she couldn't quite put her finger on.

This was a matter that Paul himself chose to question her on, a move that she thought most peculiar saying the two appeared to share much in common.

"Tell me, exactly how did you first meet that girl?" His question was directed at Josie even though Gregg was present.

"On the ferry boat crossing to Los Christianos when we docked in La Gomera!" There was no reason why she could not be truthful in her response even if she still considered it most unusual for this man to ask. "As a matter of fact she was crossing over to that place in order to deposit some of her art work and as I was on my own and she appeared to know the area she invited me to tag along with her!"

"You said her art work?"

"Yes actually she showed me some and it appeared to be rather good. Anyway having little else to do and Fern knowing the place well I tagged along with her. It was as we were returning on the journey back to the ship that I discovered that she was completely on her own and also she was sitting in the Restaurant sharing a table with people who did not share her interests. As we had a spare place at our own table at the time it seemed courteous to ask her to join us. But then as we got back to La Gomera we actually spotted you there and that was when she confessed that she had known you in the past!" Josie determined that she would tell this man nothing without at least getting some feed back from him.

"As a matter of fact I had met her in the past!" Paul seemed equally determined that whilst he wanted to know the relevant details he was not giving anything away concerning his own role in the matter. Instead he watched Fern's retreating figure before making his own excuses.

"So is that series of little interludes set to spoil the rest of our day?" It was Gregg's turn to now demand attention and so dismissing Paul Butler from her mind Josie turned with a smile to face him!

It was a two day sail back to Tenerife from those Islands so far south and yet they were to see little of Fern during that time as she had apparently chosen to eat her meals outside of the main Restaurant, which of course was a legitimate option for she was quite free to eat in the Secret Garden serve yourself cafe but the matter still left Josie feeling puzzled especially as there had been no sign of Paul Butler in that time either.

Still it was on the second of these mornings that Josie received a surprise teletext message from Frederick Hauser stating that he had been instructed to meet her by the Pyramids of Guimar when they finally arrived at Tenerife. At the time Josie felt a little perplexed for the advanced bookings to visit this place had now been finalised. She was in fact still wondering what to do about it when Gregg caught her expression even whilst she was still pondering on the feasibility of hiring a taxi to take her there but upon reflection realising she could hardly expect any taxi driver to wait for her when she didn't know exactly what time Frederick would show up and allowing the taxi to depart would find her fraught with difficulties in finding a further taxi to bring her back.

"So you have had some bad news?" He queried the paper she still held out in her hand.

"No, it is simply that I have been summoned to meet a colleague by the Pyramids at Guimar and I simply don't know how on earth I will get there and back!"

"Pyramids in Tenerife, well I suppose that is a first!"

"I had never heard of them before either but apparently there are Pyramids in Tenerife and that is the place I need to get to!"

If Gregg hadn't heard of these Pyramids before then he quickly assimilated the need.

"Then what on earth are you worrying about? I'll get a car for us to travel there in!" There was a certainty about Gregg's tone that was enough to dispel her inner fears. Yet she still felt selfish for imposing on him.

"But surely that is an imposition and moreover is hardly being fair on you! After all Frederick Hauser has to do with my employ!"

"Ah so now my opposition is this person called Frederick Hauser is it?" He was tormenting her of course until he noticed her expression. "Haven't you realised by this time that I want to be wherever you are?" He eyed her quite seriously. "Anyway who is this Frederick Hauser and what does he want? Do I need to be jealous by any chance?"

Josie smiled as she shook her head. " I don't think you have any need to be jealous. But speaking seriously I thought that I had parted company with this man for good way back on the Rhine. Still I suppose he did do me a favour back there when he rescued me from the Baron's clutches!"

Gregg's eyes opened further. "Don't tell me that I have got even more opposition in a further person then?"

She laughed as the movement of the boat sent a wall of spray up into the freshening wind. "Don't even think about it. At the time I was left under the impression that

I was proving to be quite a chore to Frederick Hauser just because my original contact at the place never showed up and consequently he felt that he had to take over the role both as my guide and guardian at that place!"

" Then in that case can I take it that I can afford to relax and save my efforts to wooing the fair damsel?"

"Well I suppose there is at least one thing both you and Helmut can thank Frederick for and that is he did pass on my father's late effects to me and that included the map that Helmut now believes to be the Holy Grail!"

"Maybe, but you have still not solved my immediate problem. We have a full days sail ahead of us before we reach Tenerife, so what are we going to do today?"

"You mean that Helmut is still not braying for your assistance?"

"I doubt it very much. But on the off chance that he does want me then I am afraid he will just have to go without. After all as you said yourself we are at sea all day and therefore I hardly consider the man needs a nursemaid to hold his hand for there is no diving involved. Plus the fact is that I now consider I have found a far better way to occupy my time. Therefore you be the judge of what it is to be. I believe there is a talk on drugs given by some narcotics expert followed by a talk on future cruises and the Chef is also giving a cookery demonstration. Alternatively we could always try walking a mile with a smile with the fitness experts, we could go golf putting, or even play a game of carpet bowls. Alternatively we could just sit here, relax and possibly enter into the realms of conversation!"

" In that case that is the option that I think I will choose. Plus the fact we need to make the best of the warm sunshine whilst it lasts because the weather report this morning said it was snowing back in England!"

"England if I need to remind you, is still a long way off. Let me refresh my memory on that one. Wasn't that the place where I first set eyes on that young lady from off the television, the one who had a charge to complete and a gun in her possession, even if she had been set up by being issued with a useless piece of armament? Yet now I find the same prim and proper madam to be a real woman and a very desirable one at that! In fact I find her desirable enough to want to spend the rest of my days with. Still I wonder whether she by any chance happens to feel the same way about me?"

She did not immediately respond for she felt her cheeks flushing a bright red and in return Gregg smiled cheekily. "I take your silence for a yes. In which case this is a matter we must discuss further in private!"

She knew full well that he was waiting for an answer from her yet Josie felt she still had much to think about. Not least in how she had managed to arrive in this situation. But then the stars were showing in their full majesty as they strolled the deck sometime later and such a scene was enough to melt any girl's heart. Indeed looking up there seemed to be so many of them that Josie wished she had acquired a little more knowledge on astronomy.

She felt his arm encircle her shoulders as she stopped to wonder at them for such a sight was not very often obvious from the U.K.

"I guess it's a rather sobering to think of so many other worlds out there. It really makes us appear quite insignificant in the order of things!" She voiced her thoughts aloud in a voice that was hardly above a whisper.

"I believe that we are very significant within the universe!" He responded thoughtfully. "Maybe those stars were placed there for a purpose, at least the sailors of old before the invention of modern equipment depended on them and I believe that we do too. For looking at them on a night like this serves to make us realise the general order of things and a phase within such an order is when a man feels that he has finally found his mate and the person with whom he is in love!"

He kissed her then, long and lingering as if he wanted to cherish this moment for all eternity and in their turn the stars peered down from out of the heavens and smiled their affirmation at such a union

Even so such ideal situations often do not last for long and Gregg sighed as he noted the appearance of Helmut on the deck.

"Surely he doesn't want me to put him to bed now!" The man at her side groaned as the figure came towards them. But strangely enough it appeared to be Josie whom Helmut was looking for.

"Josie did your father ever speak about this map, about the supposed war between Atlantis and Athens when Atlantis was rocked with earthquakes and floods before it was entirely swallowed up by the sea?"

Josie shook her head somewhat bemused and Gregg clicked his tongue impatiently. "What have you been reading up about that place now Helmut?"

"Apparently sixty five million years ago a ten kilometre meteorite crashed down in the gulf of Mexico. Oh I'm sorry, am I interrupting something?"

"Well I suppose the answer is yes to that. But what makes you think that Josie father was interested in all this?"

"The point of impact still maintains its shape on the earths crust as well as the semi circular coastline it left behind. Moreover in plate tectonics we now have the Mid Atlantic Ridge left to represent the centre of earthquakes and volcanic activity as we know such occurrences to exist and the Canary Basin as well as the Cape Verde all go to make up the mid Atlantic Ridge today!"

"I never heard my father mention anything like that!" Josie decided patience was in order because the man was obviously sincere in his findings. Patience however did not appear to be Gregg's present outstanding virtue.

"Nor would any right minded thinking individual. If that sort of reading amuses you then please keep it strictly to yourself Helmut!"

The Dutchman looked a little hurt at Gregg's tone and Josie hastened to now placate him. "Perhaps if my father had studied the subject matter as deeply as what you have yourself he would have come up with similar conclusions Helmut. But in my father's case collecting maps was only a hobby and not his true profession, so in this case I'm sorry that I cannot help you!"

At least the Dutchman looked a little more content at her words as he bade them both good night. But turning again to face Gregg she found that now some of the magic of earlier on had disappeared and consequently they finished the evening sharing a coffee!

Chapter Eight

"Tell me then exactly what do you know about this place?" Perhaps Gregg had spoken the words in order to take her mind off that forthcoming meeting as they travelled along the Los Loros route towards the Pyramids the following morning, for no doubt he could tell from her expression that a certain amount of anxiety now beset her. It was not because of their transport either for the car that he had hired had been waiting for them as soon as they had stepped ashore at Santa Cruz and there was no doubt that several envious looks had been cast in their direction as others had been forced to wait for their multiple travel means which meant that at the time Josie had been more than glad at Gregg's foresight in hiring this vehicle.

"That ancients, is that what you mean?" Perhaps Josie was trying her best to disguise the quandary that had plagued her mind ever since she had learnt of the proposed meeting with Frederick, for she still could not help but wonder what on earth this meeting entailed.

"Well the actual truth is I am afraid hard to establish but the first inhabitants of these Islands were supposed to have come from North Africa as long ago as three thousand B.C. They were reputed to have been of Neolithic stock from the Cro-Magnum area and they were tall, well built but with narrow skulls. One thing is certain however and that is the fact that this race arrived well before the Gaunches finally came in the second century B.C. Not that the later settlers came from the same place for it appears that the word Gaunche is a generalised term given to describe these settlers on Islands that apparently the ancients already knew about long before such information could be found in the writings both of Roman historians and also Ptolemy who produced a fairly accurate map of the area around 150A.D and depicted with some fear that these lands lay at the end of the world!"

"I can see that you have obviously studied your subject well Miss Craven!" Obviously Gregg seemed to be impressed or else he was still just finding a means to occupy her mind so that she could not dwell upon whatever lay ahead

"Maybe I first became interested in the subject at a time when I still believed that the Gaunches belonged to one race when in actual fact they came from vastly different cultures, in the same way as you are currently trying to take my mind off what Frederick will have to say when we arrive!"

Gregg pulled a wry face at being caught out in his well meaning deception but the site was already upon them and the person Josie had named as Frederick was waiting there for them as they arrived at this piece of recently discovered history, his timing of course being as always quite impeccable! In fact even before they had arrived at the place Josie would dearly have loved to have stopped to take a closer look at the cave houses on the way from the ship which were prehistoric in origin but still inhabited in this present era, but at the time Gregg had rightly persisted that they needed to press on to make their rendezvous at the appointed time!

From his appearance Frederick appeared pleased to see that Josie had arrived in a car and not amidst the thousands of other tourists who could possibly have caused an upset to their solitary meeting, although in all truth his eyes still held a hint of suspicion when he spotted Gregg accompanying her and his body motions conveyed that he was not totally pleased to see that she had not come here on her own.

"It's all right Frederick this is Gregg who happens to be a friend of mine!" Josie prejudged the other's mood. "You can speak in front of him for I can vouch that he poses no danger!" Josie had in her own mind immediately attempted to reassure the man whom they had just met, although from the expression on his face one could tell that she had not completely convinced him. Even so her eyes at the same time flittered around the ancient edifices for they were now currently managing to fascinate her and she determined that she would see them properly whilst she was here and ponder upon the linkage of these monuments to others found all over the world. In fact she felt she could have well done without Frederick being there at all even though it had been his command that had brought her here in the first place.

"I'm afraid that this happens to be a private matter Josie!" Frederick's response sounded stern and seemingly held within it a note of reproof almost as if he was still intent upon reminding her exactly just whom she was supposed to be working for.

"If you are now speaking of our mutual boss who is currently in a far away country then I am afraid that for my part I do not think it was entirely Kosher to play a trick on me just in order to get me to volunteer my services!" She tossed her head almost defiantly back whilst at the same time she craned her neck in an attempt to see inside the Museum where the models of the early 'reeded' boats used by one bygone race where situated and marvelled at how reminiscent they appeared to be to the Viking long boats that had appeared in later years. With all her heart she wanted to go inside now and take a closer look, an action that she was currently being denied and a measure that left her feeling more than a little displeased.

For his part Frederick meantime appeared to be a little surprised at her outburst but this in no way was to deter him from pursuing his quest. "I shouldn't be the one to have to remind you that you are not employed by the Service merely to ask questions! Neither come to that are you supposed to be here on a sight seeing expedition. You are here in fact to simply obey the orders that you will receive as well as those that have already been given to you. If you are not prepared to do that without question then perhaps you selected the wrong occupation in the first place!"

"Here, steady on!" It was Gregg who now decided to make his voice heard. "You are actually saying that Josie has no right to question the orders of the faceless ones when for no apparent reason she was directed to kill a man who was not guilty of anything. And another thing, she was also expected to use a weapon to complete this allocated task that was totally useless?"

Frederick eyed the other very carefully before he responded. "Exactly who do you purport to be Mr ---- err---- Gregg? I must say that you appear to be well versed in the methods of our Government Department as well as in the movements of Miss Craven?"

"The name if it matters to you at all is Anderson and for what it is worth I am afraid that I object to having my fiancé berated in such a manner!" His words caused Josie's face to glow for this was the second time that Gregg had referred to her as his fiancé and there was definitely something very comforting to the soul in them. It was then that she remembered the quote for the day in the ship's Times, 'let your heart guide you on!' and at the time she surely believed this to be a truth.

"You say that you are her fiancé, but as far as I understand the Department was under the impression that the girl was single and unattached Mr ---err ----?"

"So that is the reason why your Department considers that Josie can be berated, because folk believed her to be single and consequently an easy target? And at the risk of repeating myself, the name is Gregg Anderson and I, for want of a better description, am accompanying her with her consent! If you wish to learn more about me then I will also volunteer the information that I happen to be a Marine Biologist who at the present time is in the process of assisting a colleague to draw up feasibility study which has brought us to these parts! Not of course that should prove to be of any interest to you!"

His words however obviously had the other man interested. "And if I might enquire what are you drawing up a feasibility study on?"

"I was not under the impression that I worked for your beloved department Mr Hauser, nor do I imagine for one moment that you have come here to question me about my employ so consequently I hardly consider any answer to your question to be any of your business. What concerns me and the reason I am here is because I happen to care about Miss Craven's welfare!"

Frederick glanced up in the air as if he was contemplating whether to continue with this game of charades and then obviously feeling that he might still glean something out of this meeting. "Tell me then, this boat you arrived here on today. You haven't seen anyone on it who goes under the name of Fern Astor have you?" The question was of course directed at Josie but it was still Gregg who responded.

"Yes. As a matter of fact if you must know Josie happened to first meet her on a ferryboat crossing from La Gomera to this Island on one of the stops we made as we were in the process of travelling to the Cape Verde archipelago. Befriending her she then arranged for Fern to share our table in the Restaurant. I believe if I am right that she is supposed to be some sort of artist but recently we have discovered that she also enjoys cultivating the art of disappearing as well. But why have you asked? What relevance has the presence of this girl to your organisation?"

"You were brought here for a purpose Miss Craven however deceptive you believe our methods actually were!" The man totally ignored Gregg's interjection. "We would now like you to find out a great deal more about this woman whom we are interested in!"

"As far as I know she appears to be a firm friend of Paul Butler who is coincidently also now on the same cruise boat. Therefore as I believe that he is one of your boys why don't you ask him for to my mind that would make a far simpler solution?"

"Do I now detect a note of sarcasm in your voice Miss Craven? It would appear that your new found friends have initiated you into certain ways for such mannerisms were not yours when we first met on the Rhine if my memory serves me right!"

"All right then what do you want to know about Fern?" Memories of what she owed to Frederick during that sojourn came back to mind and therefore Josie decided to bite her tongue

"For a start we would like to acquaint ourselves with her contacts as well as reaching a fuller understanding as to what the girl is about. You see the initial idea was that we felt that as a member of the same sex you would stand a better chance of filtering into some sort of friendship with her and from what has already been stated it now appears that we were not far wrong in making this assumption!"

"Then it would appear that Josie was already ahead of you in doing just that!" Gregg grimaced in the speaker's direction almost indeed as if he now either resented the man barking out orders to Josie or ignoring his own comments.

"I understood that she was travelling in order to make new contacts with her art work!" Josie decided that perhaps it was better to ignore Gregg's comment less trouble ensued and thought back to her first meeting with the girl. She also remembered how at the time Fern had promised to show her these self same Pyramids, a matter that had remained at the back of her mind until this moment. Indeed she glanced over her shoulder on the off chance that the girl they had mentioned had made her way to this site after all but of course there was no one else in the near vicinity.

Frederick for his part appeared to be perhaps a little crestfallen at this explanation however. It was indeed as if he had expected Josie to be able to reveal more, yet at the same time if the man had admitted the truth he would have to have said that this assignment was becoming a positive chore to him. Indeed the very location of this meeting meant little to Frederick for he was merely obeying orders that he felt he could not question although in truth there were often times when he felt he should have done exactly that. But now he considered that his task had been completed, however unsatisfactory the results appeared to be, and he had already turned his mind onto matters that he considered to be far more important.

"Perhaps she is, or perhaps there is still more for you to find out for us Miss Craven. So Madam I will leave you with the instructions to observe the woman and then report back. You will be contacted at La Palma; I believe I am right in saying that your ship berths there. And now if you will both excuse me!"

"Just one moment before you go, just exactly what is this line of yours that enables you to fly from place to place and command others to do your bidding?"

Frederick paused for a moment as he studied the speaker before an unaccustomed smile curved his lips. "I'm afraid that there are some questions that you just do not ask Miss Craven. You see you appear to have still much to learn about the Service. Shall we just say that I am sure that I will be actively employed and also I do not feel that you need to consider it to be such a mystery as to who will be contacting you again very shortly!"

She watched as he walked away from the exhibition centre to the place where he had parked his vehicle. "So what are we supposed to do now?" It was Gregg who she now turned to for reassurance.

"Well as I guess that we have taken the time and the trouble to come and meet your little man, not that I consider meeting him was worth the trouble, but now as we are here I suggest that we now make the most of our opportunity to take a look around. I know full well that you have been dying to do that ever since we arrived for I could tell as much from that certain look in your eyes. So let's start by you telling me whether you believe that this place is genuine or a gimmick put on for the tourist trade!"

"Well I suppose the links with other pyramid structures in different parts of the world are clear enough. It was supposed to be dated at a time when according to my potted history readings, mankind generally were sun worshippers and these pyramids here appear to be well aligned to the winter and summer solstices. What puzzled me in my reading however were the tales of the men with beards and how the Spaniards were well accepted in the Caribbean because of these long hair flexes simply because the natives there claimed to have been visited by such bearded men before; men who had apparently promised that they would come back and yet these same Spaniards still wearing such facial adornments were fiercely opposed when they first came to these Islands!

"Perhaps and it is only a perhaps, the natives there recognised the bearded ones from the past because they were there own kind. And if one stops to consider the shape of those 'reeded' boats that have recently been proved to be able to withstand long distances, as for example in the Kon Tiki expedition, the Viking long boats that we know about appear to be a more modern interpretation both in shape and in the use of timber that man had found how to use!"

"Now you are living in the land of myths and legends, even if by doing so you have succeeded in taking your mind off one undesirable little man and enthralled me with your creative imagination!" Gregg smiled kindly in her direction and then as if he did not wish to hurt her feelings. "Although if on the other hand Atlantis was populated by such an advanced race or if they were extra terrestrial beings if one takes notice of Plato's description, I suppose that anything is possible. Why even the ancient worship of the sun by these ancients can be aligned in their belief in Sirius and the after life that the Egyptians postulated about. But to return to more mundane matters I guess I am feeling famished so let's return to the town and then I'll buy you a paella for to be honest with you I don't feel inclined at this moment in time to listen to the diving exploits of Helmut and Paul Butler if that is what they have been doing whilst we have been away!" Gregg swallowed after issuing the phase. He hadn't meant to mention Helmut or his interests on that day. Neither did he want to reflect on the argument that had ensued when he had refused to go diving with the man after all.

"You said that there was to be no diving here in Tenerife! I'm sorry but I have now made other arrangements!"

Helmut had shrugged his shoulders at Gregg's words. "Well I changed my mind. It seemed to be a pity to miss out on such an opportunity after all and I actually thought you would be all for it!"

"Sorry but whatever it is that you have planned then you will have to count me out. I've no intention of letting Josie down again, not after promising to take her to see those Pyramids she was on about!"

"So Josie's needs are now greater than my own? Well so be it, I'll ask Paul, he is usually willing to help out anyway!"

Maybe he should never have questioned Helmut on Paul at that stage, it was just that Josie's feelings about the man, however unfounded they might have been, kept recurring to him, plus the fact that although he knew that Paul and Helmut went back a long way, perhaps he still felt unsure in his own mind exactly why Paul Butler had come on this cruise, especially as he had joined the ship late "You never really said Helmut just why Paul turned up on this cruise?"

Helmut's expression had been unfathomable. "Perhaps it is not for me to question his line of employ. I only know Paul as a friend from the past and a damned good diver at that. His work on the other hand is secretive and I consider that its nature is none of my damned business and neither is it yours come to that. But then I suppose you have become so besotted with that girl that she is now putting ideas into your head!"

Gregg had swallowed hard. Maybe he had been wrong to question his friend's integrity, for he hadn't really meant anything by it. After all he knew full well that the two of them were old friends therefore was it possible that this outburst had been provoked because Helmut had spoken about going diving with Paul when he had refused to go himself? In truth the other man had every right to do so!

"Look I'm sorry and if it is of any use I apologise. You are probably right in what you say but at the moment I feel a little bemused about this character Josie is supposed to be meeting so I guess I wasn't thinking straight when I questioned your own motives. The point is am I forgiven for my untimely outburst?"

The two had shaken hands but now Josie had chosen to bring the subject of Helmut back again to the fore. "Maybe you should after all have gone along with them. I guess I dragged you away from something that was closer to your heart!" Perhaps after all she had sensed something of what was currently going on in his mind.

"No way! After all I chose to spend the day with you out of my own free will and I am certainly not sorry about that!"

"Well they do say that when you can see Gran Canaria from these shores it is a sure sign of rain for the following day and rain is after all supposed to make the fish bite a little more easily!"

"I thought I had already told you, I made my choice. Helmut has a companion to dive with, which is what matters, and moreover the findings for our project are more or less completed now." She wondered if his words held a tinge of disappointment in them because Helmut had asked Paul Butler to complete the dive with him, but if this existed his next words soon served to dispel such a notion! "That is why I am now suggesting that we should attempt to escape the lot of them today for after all the boat doesn't sail until midnight!"

The thought of this act now amused Josie. "You mean we can pretend to be a little like Cinderella and get back to the boat just before the bewitching hour but before all our finery disappears?"

"I mean that I am rapidly falling in love with you Josie Craven and crave your company strictly for myself. What is more I have also the distinct impression that my feelings are reciprocated!"

She blushed prettily at his words and in response he took hold of her hand almost possessively. "So am I right in my assumption? Are my feelings for you returned as your own?"

"I rather guess that they are!" Her words were mumbled as she finally admitted the truth but they were loud enough for Gregg to hear then and he bent over to kiss her in full view of the folk who were frequenting the café there!

Possibly realising that they were now drawing attention to themselves Josie persuaded him into the cinema at the centre with a film currently being shown that highlighted many of the features and linkages to other historical structures all over the world. As it was one of the latest types of cinemas, the doors closed as soon as the film began, which gave them a short respite from the outside world and thus helped to cover their embarrassment, for when the doors reopened after the film had finished at least the crowd who had witnessed that kiss and their closeness beforehand had now all gone.

They returned to Santa Cruz after touring the six stepped Pyramids orientated to the summer and winter solstices and similar to the ones found in Mexico and Mesopotamia and marvelling at the theories surrounding their origin. Gregg had asked her if she wanted to go on to visit Las Canadas and Mount Teide; but Jose had shaken her head for to have combined such visits would only have spoiled the magical effect that the Pyramids had spun around her and returning to the ship later on that night after spending some valued time together in Santa Cruz where she had felt all her in built worries dissipating in the company of the man she was beginning to love so much. They sat together for a while on the deck watching as the city throbbed to life with evening revellers. By this time theirs' was not the only cruise ship berthed there for other ships appeared to have arrived at this port from out of nowhere almost at a moment's notice whilst their passengers, anxious to experience the delights of the city had already swelled the numbers parading those famous streets. Sitting in the contrasting stillness on the deck at this hour with Gregg however seemed to be a time for reflection of that certain phrase captured for the day to 'let your heart guide you. It whispers so listen to it carefully!' and that she was content to do as his arm stole once more around her, for this was a time she never wanted to end.

It was Gregg who was the one who suddenly started and pointed towards the quay. A taxi had just pulled up alongside of the ship and a figure had emerged from it. "Guess she is leaving it a little bit late!" He glanced at his watch as they took in the figure of Fern Astor. "Wonder where she has been until this time?"

"Probably selling her art work somewhere on the Island!"

"Come off it Josie, you know full well what your friend intimated about her earlier on today!"

"But we don't really know do we? Therefore how can we say otherwise? Still as a matter of fact when I came back for my wrap earlier on whilst you returned the car I spotted her leaving the ship and I thought then that she was leaving it a little late to be going anywhere in particular at that time!"

"Then perhaps we ought to try to find out, subtly of course where she intended going: But then that is probably where a woman's touch can come into its' own. Still I'm a little surprised you didn't stop to ask her when you saw her if only to satisfy your curiosity!"

"I didn't get the chance, to tell you the truth I didn't really dare especially with the expression she was wearing on her face at the time!"

"Even so after the occasion with Helmut's papers the other day maybe we should make an effort to find out more about the woman!" She sensed an air of determination about the man, a matter that left her pondering for after all it wasn't Gregg who had been charged with that mission. On the other hand she had sensed a certain air about him since their own return and wondered whether it was because they had seen no sign of his companion since that time.

"Well one supposes Tenerife has more to tempt man than a load of pyramids!" She remembered how he had deliberately tried to force a smile when she had questioned him after he returned the car claiming that they wouldn't need it to eat out and had suggested instead a little therapeutic shopping.

As the boat was berthed quite close to the terminal buildings in the city this had ruled out a massive walk into the city itself even if the traffic and crossing the road had proved to be something of a nightmare. Surprisingly enough for such a cosmopolitan place English was not such a well-accepted language despite the fact that it was taught as a compulsory subject in all the schools and spoken avidly in the Southern coastal resorts on that Island. This was a factor that had pulled them both up short especially when they had found themselves stuck in the lift of a well known department store which had eventually deposited them in the cellar of that place, much to the consternation of the security guard there for this was forbidden territory for customers. Fortunately Gregg did possess a smattering of Spanish, enough anyway to find that they needed to press the sign SS to reach street level and not the bottom button which had appeared the most logical thing to press at the time.

"I am not as you would believe upset about Helmut's disappearance!" He had already gathered her thoughts as they sat in the open-air café on the Pez Espana during the afternoon. "I was just frightened that I would find him sulking on board when we got back! I should have realised that he has probably gone somewhere with Paul, perhaps the two of them had a yen to travel to the South of the Island where there are ample diving schools for them to peruse and where conditions are right for that sort of activity. After all they will have plenty of time to do that and get back before the boat is due to sail!"

"I still don't quite understand this sudden affiliation between the two of them though!" Josie had wrinkled up her nose for try as she would she could not feel comfortable when that man Paul Butler was around.

"I thought that you already knew. Actually the two of them go back for some considerable time. Apparently they both attended the same courses when they first started diving. An unlikely friendship, I agree with you on that. After first meeting however they went their own way in life for years and I don't actually think they met up again until we were on this cruise. Still taking in your present negative expression I suppose it is no good telling you to forget the thoughts that are currently bombarding your mind but I am sure the man has no intention of trying to harm you. The point now is, shall we try to forget about them now and instead think about ourselves?"

"For example?"

"Why do you always want explanations? Instead let's start by you telling me what I need to do in order to convince you of my feelings, and remember when you decide to give me the answer that I want that no one else is involved in this. It is just the two of us!"

"Somehow I guess I have always managed to fight off ever getting myself in this position before. You see I was always determined to remain solo!"

"And now, has anything happened to make you change your mind?"

She nodded. "I think perhaps that it has. Against my better judgement initially I admit but something that I now find that I can no longer deny!"

"In that case do you think I stand a chance?" His voice sounded almost pleading in its inflection as she surrendered to the motions of her heart.

"I thought I had already given you an answer to your question!" She spoke slowly for such words did not issue easily from her lips but Gregg looked gratified with her response as if he himself now desired some reassurance.

Even so the late appearance of Fern now served to promote Josie into taking action and much to Gregg's surprise the girl jumped up. "I suppose I could try to catch her by the lifts!" She now spoke almost determinedly, an act that perhaps took her companion aback.

"Don't tell me the Department has motivated you into acting so quickly?" For a moment Josie wondered whether a hint of sarcasm had entered her companion's voice. She supposed in a sense that she couldn't blame the man but her sense of curiosity had still not been removed.

"Please Gregg, call it curiosity if you like but I need to find out!"

He sighed somewhat dejectedly as she made to leave and Josie found that she was now fighting with something that resembled a guilt complex for in truth she would far rather have stayed with this man at that time. Even so having made the move she found that she had been right in her assumption and found Fern just about to embark into the lift that she had been waiting for on the embarkation floor

"We went to see the Pyramids today!" It was one way of opening the conversation she supposed, although at the time she was at a loss at the way she could achieve the feat she had set out to accomplish. Still her words appeared to have some affect on the girl for Josie witnessed a look of abject horror passing across the other girl's face as she suddenly stopped in her tracks.

"Oh I am sorry, I guess I forgot!" Perhaps Josie informed herself this was the nearest she would ever get to obtaining some sort of apology from this girl for breaking a promise. "I guess I was completely tied up in my art work to the exclusion of everything else!"

"Actually Gregg drove me to the Pyramids and you were right, the place was well worth a visit!" She witnessed a tinge of curiosity in the other girl's face at the mention of Gregg's name and at least prided herself that she had caught the other girl's interest.

"Glad you managed to find them then!" At least these were the only words she used to now acknowledge Josie's response.

"But you mentioned your art work, did you find something to inspire you there on the Island then?" Josie attempted to change the subject matter.

"I managed fairly well yes thank you!" She noticed now that the girl clutched her folder even more tightly to her form as if she was afraid of anyone seeing the contents.

"Then why not share the subject matter that you managed to achieve. I'm interested in your work for after all you appear to be very accomplished, far more than what I am myself?"

Perhaps however even Josie had underestimated the other's reaction to her words for immediately clutching the folder even more tightly to her chest Fern responded to this request almost churlishly. "My work on the project is still not complete so if you don't mind I'll keep it to myself for the time being!" Her tone now was adamant and Josie became aware that there was no way that Fern intended to loosen her hold on that folder

"In that case think nothing of it, I was merely interested in your work that is all! After all I have seen some of the work you have produced in the art class on board!"

"But not tonight I think!" And with these words Fern made no bones about leaving her and catching the lift that had arrived by this time on the deck thus leaving Josie to stand forlornly by the closed lift doors.

Josie was in fact still pondering on the matter when she realised that Gregg had followed her after all. "Well, and if it is not too rude a question what did you manage to find out? I must admit I was surprised to see that your friend Frederick had motivated you into action so quickly!"

She pulled a face as she turned towards him. "Nothing I'm afraid, the lady does not appear to be in the mood for talking even about her art work tonight!"

"Still I suppose one ought to commend you for trying anyway. Who knows tomorrow she might possibly have a change of heart and show you the contents of her portfolio after all!" So Gregg had witnessed the conversation after all! "But as she has gone now I think such matters will have to wait for some time for I do believe we have some unfinished business to attend to ourselves: In which case shall we try to forget about your man from the Ministry and his so called demands?"

She nodded in return and after uttering these words Gregg grasped her arm almost possessively as he made to lead her back again towards the lifts and this time Josie did not object, not even when they reached the companionway that housed her cabin

She knew he had been standing close behind her but now she became even more conscious of his presence as wisps of air wafted the delicious sense of masculine hormones onto her nasal membranes. She heard his breath almost laboured as his body now moved ever closer to her own as if demanding the entwinement of their souls. The hairs on the back of her neck began to bristle under the command of his breath until his arms finally rested upon her forcing her to turn to take the full embodiment of his lips upon her own. It was a kiss that held a thousand promises and aroused a zest to understand the true meaning of life. It was a seal that neither of them could break. Her cabin door was already open and therefore it now appeared only natural that they should move back through that aperture to the comfort of the bed whilst Gregg for his part possibly sealed their pact by kicking the door well and truly shut so that the eyes of the outside world could no longer play witness to the passion that was now to ensue between them as their bodies entwined together as one!

* * * *

Chapter Nine

Josie wondered what Frederick would have said if he had known where she was to spot Fern next, for in truth there had been no sighting of the woman at the dining table, nor had she shown any further remorse at forgetting, if that is what had really happened, to show Josie the Pyramids as she had once offered, apart that was from the remark she had made when they had passed in the companionway the previous night. Not that Josie had attached too much importance to this at the time for she herself had been fully occupied with Gregg. Which was of course was why she now felt that she needed to get away on her own on the following day without mentioning the fact to him, for she had determined after spending that second night with the bloke, that this affair with Gregg had got to stop.

In essence she had previously booked a place on the coach to take her to see the Caldera De Taburiente on the Island of La Palma earlier on in the voyage and therefore she had said little about this fact to the man who now appeared determined to be her escort. This was indeed to prove true when she managed to catch a glimpse of his face after learning of her proposed departure and she could not help but notice that he looked anything but pleased with the idea of her going without him.

"But you could have mentioned this before!" It was the time for confessions but then Josie had hers ready and waiting for hadn't she been pondering over the matter for some time?

"Actually I booked to go on this trip when we first boarded!" At least that part was the truth. "I actually felt that there was something determinedly eerie about the description of the place and I really wanted to see it for myself! Plus at that time I hardly visualised that we would become an item during this trip." Perhaps however she had suddenly changed her mind about going on her own for she then continued, "I suppose that whilst it isn't for me to press you on the matter, but if you really do want to come then you could always go and see if there are any spare places left instead of sitting there pulling your face like that!" With the take up of the other excursions she doubted very much at the time that there would be any spaces left but at least she felt that this suggestion did help to absolve some of the guilt she was now feeling!

"Well I must say that is very nice coming from you and by the way I was not pulling my face. I simply don't feel in the mood of losing sight of you!"

"In that case I suppose I could come with you to Reception and see if they have any spare seats on the coach!" Of course at the time she truly believed that there would not be any, but with a bad grace he persisted in going anyway. Indeed she had swallowed hard when she watched him hand over his card to pay for a seat before finally decided that whatever would be had to be after all. Yet much as Josie herself wanted to visit this place after all she had heard about it she still felt at that time that she would have much preferred to have been on her own with time to spare to collect her thoughts together on what was actually happening to her.

He gave some indication of his feelings as they crossed the gangway together. "You didn't seriously think that I would have let you go on your own did you? I'm not taking any chances of having someone else attaching himself to you whilst my back is turned!" He grabbed her hand and gave it a squeeze as they waited to get on the coach and Josie felt a complete eel for her earlier thoughts even if the thought did cross her mind to wonder if Gregg had been referring to Frederick being around! Yet even so it now seemed comforting to have him here with her as they viewed the site of thc Lady of the Snows with its obscure history and they listened as they were told that this was a place where pilgrims were expected to pause for a while before embarking on their journey into the interior and pray for a safe return.

But this was a journey that would take them through the tunnel from the Eastern part of the Island where they had docked at the port and where the weather seemed to be a little overcast, to the Western side where the sun shone and the white shield of cloud found that it could not transgress the heights of those mountains, thus leaving behind the Canaria Pines to suckle the moisture from the clouds that lay there for their own sustenance.

Eventually sitting on the low stonewall overlooking the ravine which many claimed was a bottomless pit although the guide informed them rather knowledgeably that it was merely a 6300ft drop, and close to the parking area which was cleared of trees, the morning sun now beat pleasantly down on them; something which proved to be totally different from the way it acted along those walks in the more shaded parts of this area and where the ramblers would choose one of walks of varying difficulties according to their standard, some of which led past marks of the ancients carved in the rocks. Yet these walkers unlike the coach travellers were kitted out to meet such experiences and regarded these coach travellers, garbed in holiday gear as being something of eccentrics.

Sat there Josie mused that this surely must be the most beautiful part of the Island for this was a place where one could afford to extend ones thoughts in perfect tranquillity. Now she regretted her former attitude to having Gregg's presence there for surely his company made this journey complete whilst a the same time she paused to marvel at how the vegetation had grown around and within this hole in the centre of the earth that basked in its silence! Even so this very peace was shortly to be disturbed when from out of one of the cars that had drawn up in the parking spaces a little distance from where they were sat a woman alighted, glancing at her watch and obviously appearing more than a little perturbed because the person she had arranged to meet had not yet arrived. It was Gregg who drew Josie closer to the coach where they could not be seen for Fern was openly flapping an enveloped document in her hand as if she was anxious to be parted from it!

The girl did not have to wait for long and the others from the coach had still not returned from their preamble following their tour guide, when a second car arrived. This one appeared to be driven by a man of Middle Eastern descent who eyed all onlookers with something that resembled suspicion before he moved across to where Fern was poised. What words were spoken between the two of them it was quite impossible to decipher but the meeting was brief before the man left after exchanging envelopes with Fern and sped back in his car into the shadows from whence he had emerged

"Now do you think that was art work she was selling?" Gregg knew even before he uttered the words that this was not the case.

"In an envelope? Never---it was certainly something other than that!" Perhaps for one moment Josie took him seriously

"Look what she is doing now!" He murmured as he pointed towards the girl, for after taking a quick look around and believing that she was still unobserved Fern had started to open the envelope to reveal its contents. Even from where they were, still shielded by the side of the coach, there could be no mistake that the envelope contained Euros. "It almost looks as if it is payment for services rendered!" Gregg now put her own thoughts into words and Josie felt glad that she had managed to take those two snapshots, one of Fern with the open envelope containing the Euros and the earlier one of the

Middle Eastern gentleman who in turn had scanned the contents of the envelope handed to him, possibly to make sure whether his money had been handed over for something worthwhile.

"And not for art work either!" Josie breathed. But then almost as quickly as she had arrived for this meeting Fern had already left in the same taxi that had brought her. "I just hope the photos come out O.K although I suppose it will be impossible to decipher what the envelope she gave him contained!"

"There are such things as enlargements you know. I would have thought that the people who are employing you would be good at such things!"

Still engrossed in her own thoughts Josie ignored his words "Still what I can't quite understand is why she chose to come all this way to carry out such business. I certainly don't think she had an eye for the natural beauty of the place!"

"Perhaps if you think about it one could consider that this place could make an ideal drop off zone!" Gregg mused. "After all apart from the hikers who do not tarry in the place for long before they don their gear and set off, and an odd coach load of tourists who in the main are all keen to follow the guide less they miss out on something, who else would you expect to find here in this remote spot?"

"Well it appears that he comes here for a start!" Gregg followed her gaze. In a scene that resembled something one could expect to see in a far-fetched stunt in some dramatic film, they watched as one man holding onto a long pole slid down the rocky terrain. Landing on the footpath where the walkers had recently passed by, he then paused only long enough for them to catch a glimpse of his attire with those corduroy breeches, an alpine type of trilby hat and also wearing other expensive clothing before he again lowered his pole this time down the side of the ravine and promptly descended down it at great speed.

"That is a La Palma tradition!" By this time their guide had reappeared possibly because her followers were beginning to feel the cold stinging their flesh on her proposed walk and she had caught on to their feeling of distraction. "In Spain they would call him a 'Salto del Pastor'. I do not know the English translation for that. We do not see them very often for apparently they are in a very exclusive club here on the Island that attempts to preserve an ancient way of getting from place to place on this mountainous terrain. A habit that was born at a time when there were no roads here for them to travel along. The Canary Islands may be linked together in many ways but each one has its own separate traditions, like the whistling language on La Gomera for example. Recently Archaeological studies have shown that the zone was once inhabited by a pastoral society using Neolithic materials. Humans as such have indeed been present here in the Caldera for at least two thousand years. We have our own name for the ancients. On this Island we call them the Benahories. But changing the subject I notice you did not come with us on the walk?"

"My legs ached!" Gregg pulled a face and the guide laughed at his expression.

"I see, but then I suppose it is also a tradition for the young to want to escape on their own! I believe this is especially when there happens to be love in their eyes!"

Josie blushed and the guide laughed again almost caringly. "But now I think we will all get into the coach and we will go to the Visitors Centre here in the park. There you will be able to see a short film of how this Island was first formed and why the clouds still haunt the Caldera from the spine of the mountain that governs us as well as the subterranean caves!"

"Speaking of those caves, I did hear said that someday the Island is destined to split into two and one half will fall into the sea causing a massive Tsunami!" This time it was Gregg who had shown an interest.

The guide pulled a face at his words " What you heard is true but not for many years one hopes although it is also true that the sea is currently undermining our very foundations. The consequent depression that is forming is quite obvious from the sea off the Northern part of the Island. But on the other hand we are doing our best to try to defeat such natural forces for as long as it is possible. But during our visit to the Centre there will be an opportunity for you to see for yourselves something of our origins and what serves to make this Island a Biosphere Reserve, including the numerous waterfalls that appear to arise half way up the cliffs and man's more recent addition to human habitation in the form of the Astrophysics laboratory!"

In truth the theatre was a revelation but at least unlike its cousin at the pyramids the doors to the place did not close and lock during the performance and therefore one was free to come and go at any time according to one's wishes. To go and wander around the Botanical gardens where there were species from many different continents all apparently thriving right here on this Island. Quite a sobering thought if one considered how plant life had adjusted to immigration long before man had found a need for his 'reeded' boats. But from Josie's point of view she was far more interested in trying to establish who exactly a certain character was who had taken it upon himself to wander into that theatre and then to leave again for to her mind the figure resembled that of Frederick Hauser.

From the bright sunlight that had comfortingly bathed their flesh whilst they had been in the National Park a cloud formation surrounded Santa Cruz de la Palma that afternoon. They had watched as it slowly formed from the Mirador de la Conception, a vantage point overlooking the city and the place where Josie subconsciously slipped her hand into Gregg's as the peace of this Island, especially when compared with its more boisterous neighbour, engulfed them just like the mist that was currently coming down from off those mountains was rapidly obscuring the city. They had seen no further sign of Fern but this fact hardly seemed to matter as Gregg in response to the scene bent his head to kiss her, his lips now lingering on her own like the mist that had been brought here by the trade winds. It was only when they heard the clearing of someone's throat behind them that the two of them broke apart and Josie realised she had not been mistaken when she had thought she had caught a glimpse of a certain figure back in that theatre.

"Don't let me stop you!" The words sounded almost scornful to her ears. "But I did promise you would be contacted on this Island. Have you any more details to report on the girl or have you been far too busy occupied to have borne that task in mind?" He glanced in Gregg's direction but this time he didn't really appear to mind the man's presence.

"If you are Frederick then I believe that Josie has something to tell you!" Perhaps Gregg was now taking full advantage of the situation for Frederick appeared surprised that it was he who had responded the first and therefore Josie hurriedly told him of what they had witnessed up in the Caldera.

Frederick Hauser pursed his lips. "It is as we surmised! You said that you have taken photographs?"

Josie nodded as she fished out her camera. "I don't know whether the contents of the envelopes will show up well!" She passed it to him almost automatically.

"I think you had better allow us to decide that!" He made to pocket the camera.

"But that has my holiday snaps on the disk as well!" Noting his intention Josie made to object.

"Holiday snaps Miss Craven? I wasn't aware you had been sent here on holiday?"

"Just a minute ----!" Gregg now made to intercede.

"Ah the debonair fiancé again, but then surely you must have realised by this time that the light of your eyes has a mission to complete, which if these photographs are what I must assume that they are, she has managed to go some way towards!"

"Maybe it would help all concerned if you were a little more specific on what this is all about!"

"I'm afraid one does not question the work of the Service Mr Anderson, isn't it? But then even you must be well aware of the national threat from terrorism. But I have already said more than enough. You need not worry Miss Craven, your holiday snaps, as you so delicately put it, are perfectly safe and will be returned to you when the mission is completed!"

"But what else is this girl supposed to do in order to satisfy you? After all you have now got the evidence to implicate Fern Astor in your little melodrama if what you suspect is correct and I do not think that the girl was being paid by someone who was appreciative of her art work!"

"Do you really believe the cover story she is currently proclaiming about trading art work Mr Anderson? No your task Miss Craven is to continue observing our suspect to see if there are any more gems of wisdom that you can provide us with, and you will do this without questioning your orders yourself or getting your boy friend to question for you. And now I will bid your good day for I can see that your guide is already agitating to get going less she arrives back at the ship later than what is schedule!"

He had gone before either of them could raise any objections. Simply vanished into thin air as if he had never been there at all and indeed if it had not been for the loss of her camera Josie would have doubted that he had been present and that the whole episode had been but a figment of her imagination. But then a second person had been with her at the time and he also had witnessed the man's presence. Both of them were indeed full of thought as they re-boarded the coach to take them back again to the ship.

When they returned neither Helmut nor Paul were anywhere in sight, a point that was difficult for Gregg to reconcile as Helmut had appeared non too pleased at his own proposed departure that morning.

"You now appear to be so besotted with the girl that you have conveniently forgotten our own purpose in undertaking this expedition!" He had most definitely scowled when Gregg had related his intentions.

"Why, for you can hardly say that this place lends itself to the art of diving and in any case I thought that you had already sufficient enough data that you required for your dissertation?"

"I had presumed, possibly incorrectly, that we were partners in this expedition. This concept, as far as I am concerned, hardly marries itself to the idea of making up a threesome in order to satisfy your male hormones!"

"And I was under the distinct impression that you were the one who had found another diving soul mate in Paul Butler. Therefore if I wish to satisfy a yearning on Josie's part to see something of this Island I am afraid that I do not consider that I have totally isolated you!"

Helmut had sloped off at the time on these words and therefore he had obviously found something better to occupy his time when they had arrived back at the ship, therefore Josie and Gregg found that they still had a little stolen time together to talk about the day, and consequently they sat on the deck whilst the more energetic passengers swam in the pool, and they laid back in order to enjoy the peaceful tranquillity of an afternoon by the harbour in Santa Cruz de la Palma.

Toying with Gregg's binoculars they must have been sat there for half an hour or so when through these glasses Jose spotted the car that was now returning in their direction past the army base up on the hill, and as it drew closer along the promenade that lay at that end of the city she also spotted that this was indeed the same car which they had spotted Fern arriving at the Caldera in earlier on that day. Gregg sensed her bristle.

"What is it now?" He appeared a little concerned after what had recently happened.

"Maybe I am wrong but I could swear that is the same car we spotted Fern using earlier on today that is now apparently returning to the ship past that army base over there!"

"I certainly don't know how you can see that from this distance!" Then noticing she had been using the glasses he took them from her to peer through them himself. "Maybe you are right in your assumption after all. Still upon reflection I suppose she has to return to the ship in some way for according to my watch we are almost due to sail anyway for we have not got a full days stay here!"

Josie did not respond, for although her heart already belonged to Gregg she still had other matters to successfully resolve for the sake of her father's memory. Yet Gregg had been right on one issue, the ship was now ready to leave the port.

The swirling clouds had now all but vanished into the Caldera with its massive depth as the boat nosed its way from the quayside and towards the blue skies that lay ahead. A ray of sunshine currently glistening on the water served to turn the waves now into an azure blue as the ship's engines throbbed beneath their feet and the small resort of Los Cancajos beamed out a welcoming greeting. The deck where they were sat, which until recently had enjoyed a sleepy siesta now sprang into life with those who had been waiting for the vessel to sail and the Island of La Gomera appeared yet again from out of the mist. Finally all the Islands, which had originated as the tips of volcanoes pushed up from the floor of the Atlantic by the movement of the earth's crust, were to disappear almost indeed as if they were but patches of twilight in the sea of forthcoming darkness as the daylight began to wane

In truth perhaps she should not have been so surprised when it was Paul Butler who made a point in questioning her on Fern's movements after watching the two of them follow the girl's progress as she had returned to the ship. Yet to all intents and purposes she had previously considered Paul Butler and Fern Astor to be something of an item and therefore this coupled with the fact that she still did not feel able to trust the man she therefore she felt reluctant to say anything. But it was Paul who had waited until he spied an opportunity to draw her to one side and out of the hearing of the others, for Gregg had spied Helmut and seemed anxious now to catch him for his own reasons.

"I was watching you and I must say you appeared to be very interested as you watched Fern Astor returning to the ship this afternoon?"

"And why shouldn't I have been. The girl had left it late in returning and therefore I was worried in case she did not make it back before we were due to sail!"

"But of course!" He did not appear convinced by her words and for a moment she did wonder whether this was a fit of pique on his part because Fern had not taken him into her confidence before she had left that morning for whatever reason. "But if I am correct I believe that you yourself went to the Caldera this morning? Did you find the conditions there pleasant and to your liking?"

Josie's eyes narrowed. She knew full well that the man was after something and as far as she was concerned he could go and whistle. "As a matter of fact I found them to be very pleasant. In fact I pity those who decided to stay on this side of the Island and consequently forfeited the sun!" Her tongue clicked irritated by this man who now tried to exert a certain charm over her.

"And did you by any chance see your charming dining companion whilst you were on the Island?"

"No doubt you are well aware where she has been Mr Butler considering that you appear to be well acquainted with both her and her movements yourself. I am indeed surprised that you did not accompany her on whatever expedition she had in mind?"

"I would have thought that my reasons would have been quite obvious to you Miss Craven. I presume you met Frederick Hauser at the Pyramids in Tenerife yesterday. Well the general idea was that we would not attempt to tread on your toes in your own mission for you see we considered that perhaps a woman has the means to discover quite succinctly what a member of her own sex happens to be engaged in!"

"As far as I am concerned Mr Butler, Fern Astor is only concerned and always has been in her art work!"

"By that you are saying that you did not see her meeting anyone on the Island today?"

"I am afraid that I really cannot see what business it is of yours Mr Butler as to whether I saw Fern Astor or not. I myself went to the Caldera to enjoy the vista, therefore perhaps you ought to ask your friend for yourself whether she went there to peddle her art work or not! After all you are the one who appears to share her confidence!"

"Perhaps I ought to remind you Miss Craven who is actually employing you and the task you were asked to complete for them!"

"If I remember correctly, the only task I was given to complete was to eliminate the man who was responsible for my father's death and he is apparently now standing in front of me!"

"But I thought that matter had already been resolved between us. My only involvement in the case of your father was in attempting to go to the man's assistance after he fell!"

"So is that the reason why my initial contact in Koblenz failed to show at the appointed venue because you had gone to his assistance as well?" Josie was angry, a factor illuminated by the flare of colour that now lit up her cheeks. Still at least she had the satisfaction of noting that the man in front of her looked a little more chastened as a result of her verbiage. Yet at the same time this person was not willing to completely give up on the task he had set himself.

"Do you think you could possibly consider forgetting the Rhine and what happened there for the time being and concentrate instead on the events of today?"

"You haven't said yet why you did not go ashore yourself?"

"I thought you understood that my reason was fairly obvious. If I had gone ashore then I might possibly have jeopardised any meeting taking place between Fern Astor and her contact. That was the reason why, although my orders were to cultivate the girl as far as possible, your own input was required on this occasion!"

Josie swallowed hard, still not convinced that she ought to reveal anything to this man. On the other hand Frederick had inferred that she ought to be able to trust the man and perhaps it was a moment's inflexion that allowed her now to continue. "As a matter of fact she did meet a person at the Caldera and envelopes were exchanged. As far as I am aware the one that was passed to Fern contained money, Euro notes I believe although of the amount I have no idea. The one that Fern passed to the man, I am afraid I have no idea what that contained. Quite possibly it was some of her artwork after all! Anyway even the camera found that rather difficult to interpret!"

"You mean that you managed to get a picture. That is excellent for no doubt the boys in the lab will be able to make some sense out of it. And the person whom the girl met—Are there any words you can use to describe him?"

"At a guess I would have said he was of Middle Eastern origin although trying to depict the nationality of anyone in today's society can prove to be difficult!"

"Thank you Miss Craven for actually you have been most helpful. Maybe one should consider that the Department did a rather smart job when they enlisted your assistance after all. It's just a pity that you didn't show the same aptitude when you were at University! I have now only one more question, do you happen to have your camera with you now?"

This man positively infuriated her. Still she thought that possibly she would be able to see something of her revenge when he asked for the photographs. "I am so sorry but you see Frederick took my camera, but I thought you already knew that!"

Paul appeared to start on her words and yet the expression that appeared on his face when he heard this was now enough to make her silently chuckle. "You gave the camera to Frederick Hauser?" If Josie had initially issued the matter as a mark of triumph she was now surprised to see the expression on Paul Butler's face.

"That is what I said. Rather he took my camera with all my holiday snaps intact and not just the relevant ones!" Perhaps the thought of losing her camera in such a manner was still annoying her. "But then I suppose that as Frederick happened to be my contact and the one seeking some indictment of Fern Astor it was only a natural reaction!"

"Yet you were still mistaken in doing that I am afraid!"

"I'm sorry but I fail to agree with you on that score Mr Butler, plus the fact is, if you are both working for the same Department the matter of which of you has the camera should be quite irrelevant!"

"You say irrelevant? I think not Miss Craven, but then one supposes that you could hardly be expected to sift through your memory bank to arrive at that conclusion. After all you perform much better on the stage!"

Josie walked away from the man now positively furious and she was still in this frame of mind when Gregg spotted her and left Helmut to return to her side.

"So what happened?" Gregg had already sensed that there was something obviously very wrong. "What did the man say to you that has obviously upset you?"

"Oh let him be!" Josie tried to shrug off her concern unwilling to burden Gregg with her problem. "At least I suppose he didn't get his hands on the photographs!"

"You really don't trust Paul Butler, even now, do you?"

"I'm sorry but I can't!" Her tone was adamant. "I'd also like to know how the hell he managed to be on this cruise in the first place not to mention how he was regarded so highly as to give port lectures!" Her mind had now flitted back to the first time she had realised that he was on the boat.

"The answer to your first query is simple. Paul Butler just happens to be a long-standing friend of Helmut's. Therefore when he realised that Helmut was undertaking this expedition he asked to join us at La Gomera and fortunately there was some cabin space for him!"

"It is surprising just how many people appear to have boarded at La Gomera!" She was still sceptical but nevertheless Gregg now paid little attention.

"As Paul also happened to be something of an authority on the Cape Verde Islands, having visited them before and also having read up about them, the people in the office here thought it would be a good idea if he would share some of this information at a port lecture, always providing that he was willing and when he was approached Paul agreed! Does that satisfy your inbuilt curiosity?"

"But you never said before ----?" Now it was her turn to query.

"That is probably because I didn't know at the time until Helmut informed me, speaking of who I believe he is over there and currently beckoning me!"

Gregg's attention was now obviously diverted by the arrival of Helmut who still wanted to commandeer him and thus Josie turned to make a quick exit leaving the two of them together!

Her mind still full of what had transpired Josie made for her cabin her eyes now welling with tears for it appeared to her that whatever she did was apparently wrong in the eyes of the establishment and in her present mood she wished with all of her heart that she was back on the set of that T.V. soap which at least provided some comfort for her.

At first she wasn't aware of that tapping on the door until his voice arrested her and dabbing her eyes as best she could in a veiled attempt to dry her tears she opened it to see Gregg stood there now obviously concerned by the figure he was facing.

"O.K. What's the matter then, out with it?"

"Nothing, my eyes are tired I think!"

"And is that why you have been crying then. Don't lie Josie I know something is still bugging you!"

She knew then that Gregg would demand the truth and therefore she expounded on her meeting with Paul more fully and in faltering tones whilst he in turn pulled a wry face before inviting himself in. "So you have finally let the man get at you and there was I firmly believing that wc had spent a most successful day dealing with the affairs of Her Majesty's Secret Service!"

"Personally he left me feeling that I must surely be an abject failure in any service!"

"That is nonsense and you know it. You obeyed instructions; you reported what had transpired to Frederick as requested; what more could be expected of you?"

"I appear to have done the wrong thing in allowing Frederick to take my camera. Not that I had any option at the time for I didn't particularly want to part with a disk that contained my holiday snaps!"

"Perhaps I should go and find Paul now and try to sort the mater out for you. After all I can't see how it matters who got hold of the damning photographs if damning they were, for both Paul and Frederick work from the same source!"

She knew full well that Gregg was ready to chase the matter up but she stayed him. This time around she wanted no one else to fight her battles. "Leave it alone Gregg, I guess I just allowed myself to become upset over trivialities!"

"That is probably because this is not the right line of work for you to be undertaking in the first place. Not to place too fine a point on the issue you are far too sensitive a person to mix with those who have no feelings!"

"But I owed it to my father's memory!"

"And I considered that matter had already been resolved. Your father slipped Josie. He wasn't pushed by anyone out there in the region of the Rhine. My argument is that you should have been informed of the truth right from the start and not co-opted into this arrangement!"

"Now I am afraid it is a little late in the day for me to co-opt out of this one. I appear to be right up to my neck in it!"

"But after this there will be no more occasions will there? What are you going to tell them when you get back home?"

"I've already decided I will ask them to take back their shilling!" She forced a smile.

"That is perhaps the most sensible idea you have come up with tonight. Speaking of which I do believe we have some unfinished business to carry on with!" He cupped her chin with his hands and gazed into her eyes with a look the served to banish all her outstanding doubts of the day, at least on a temporary basis! "But first I believe it is time for us to eat and then possibly relax with a drink and listen to some comforting music by which time perhaps your thoughts will have returned to a more amenable present!"

He held out his hand to help her up and she took hold of it realising yet again how comfortable she felt with this man. "Remember that tomorrow we have a day at sea and a chance therefore to put all distasteful thoughts to the back of our mind and just concentrate on being us, without interruptions too I might add!"

This scenario sounded perfect and consequently such thoughts brought a smile back again to her face.

"And that Miss Craven I conclude is very much better!" His smile now brought comfort to her thoughts and helped to ease away her feelings of ineptitude as they made their way back to the scene of the living together!

★ ★ ★ ★

Chapter Ten

Maybe it was indeed an omen of things yet to come when a storm blew up out of seemingly nowhere as they sailed the Atlantic that night. A storm moreover that was predicted to last until they reached their final port of call, which was Lisbon. For his part the Captain of the vessel had announced that he would try his best to guide the vessel as close as it was possible to the shore once they reached the Spanish mainland. In such conditions therefore one might have expected to find the decks deserted with the folk returning to the cabins with the malady of the sea, but the truth lay far from that for the passengers decided to throng the public areas instead as they were now unable to enjoy the fresh air life! Yet the day, despite the weather and as Gregg had previously intimated, was to be spent with the purpose of achieving sheer enjoyment and trying to forget other matters and with the activities that had been planned this promised to be something well within their grasp. Thus when Josie slid out of bed that morning she glanced at the still sleeping figure of Gregg with some amusement as she deliberately wafted a tissue across his face simply to torment him.

"Come back to bed woman!" The voice sounded almost gruff in its response as she felt him catch hold of her arm but in sheer amusement at his reaction she tormented him still further by running the fingers of her free hand through his hair.

"Sorry but it's time to rise! Breakfast remember, before we make our plans for this evening!"

He grumbled but obliged giving her a wry grin as he did so for that evening, possibly as an attempt by the crew to spread the icing upon the cake, it was scheduled to be the British night and therefore they both realised that it would soon be easy to be caught up in the furore of people visiting the shops on board to equip themselves with the appropriate gear for this special occasion.

Nevertheless breakfast appeared to be a solitary affair for them for neither Helmut nor Fern were present in the Restaurant not that Gregg minded, indeed he appeared to welcome the fact of being able to share breakfast with her on his own without interruptions as well as the fact that this afforded him the opportunity to discuss what they were going to wear for the festivities that evening.

For her part after finally persuading herself to visit those shops that were temptingly situated on the Main Deck, Josie decided to settle on a red tee shirt with a blue and white cardigan over a pair of jeans. Perhaps it was not the most flamboyant of costumes but it suited her in her current mood, even if Gregg decided there and then to plant a Union flag into her hands.

"Look I have no intention of going dressed like Britannia!" She objected to this act but by this time she was laughing at the man's antics.

"No doubt others will do that for you!" He pointed towards some of the gear that other passengers were currently buying. "But then I suppose the photographers will be out in full force tonight and therefore perhaps it is a case that they are willing to do anything which will at least secure them some footage on the video that is being taken! Even Helmut said that he is contemplating going as King Neptune, the idea being that Britain rules the seas etc or at least I suppose one could state that it did at one time!"

To add to the scene Gregg deliberately set one of the British helmets on her head to accompany the flag he had placed in her hand. "Now you can go as a definite Britannia!" He eyed his handiwork, which resulted in a measure that succeeded in dissolving the pair of them in uncontrollable laughter and they were still in this frame of mind when Helmut chose to pass. Moreover it could be said that the newcomer merely snorted with something that could easily be described as disgust at the sight of the pair of them dressed in this fashion.

"Oh come of it Helmut. After all this is all in aid of having a good laugh and surely that never did anyone any harm. Anyway now you have finally got up from your slumbers what do you fancy going as? Come on let's see you choose a costume of some description! I assured

Josie here that you were contemplating going as King Neptune!"

"I can assure you that I will not be there!" The other man drew himself up to his full height displaying something that resembled complete disdain at what he now termed as playing at some game of charades. "I find that I have far more interesting things to involve myself in than having to resort to infantile games!"

He made to push past them and Gregg felt compelled to exchange a somewhat bemused glance with Josie. "Oh let him be then. Perhaps if the truth is known he is objecting to the fact that he isn't English!"

The expression of disbelief now on Gregg's face caused Josie to laugh again as she allowed him to draw her into one of the lounges. "To change the subject, I think that I said it before but laughter suits you Josie. And laughter is a something that I would like to cultivate for you so that it stays with you for the rest of your life. Upon that subject we need to talk. What would you say if I told you that I had been offered a job in charge of several experimental fish farms in the North of England? Not only that but to help in overseeing the restocking of some of our rivers in that area with their natural inhabitants now that they are largely free of pollution!"

"And that is what you want to do?" She had previously wondered about his line of employ once they were back at home.

"The answer to that rather depends on you. Oh I admit that I am getting a little tired of being a University boffin and the prospect of having my own company holds quite a distinct appeal, but then I don't think I could bury myself anywhere without having a companion by my side. There is quite a good choice of locations where one could live within easy travelling distance of the various sites including the Lake District if that happens to appeal to you. So what do you think?"

Josie remained momentarily silent as she pondered two things from side to side in her head believing that her thought pattern must surely be heard, as matters within her brain seemed to bounce from side to side causing a cacophony of sound upon her cranium. But perhaps the first thing that occurred to her and propounded her thoughts was that Gregg had never mentioned anything about marriage, all he had in fact said was that he just required a companion, and the second thing was the fact that she was still under contract to the television drama company. Did she really want to give up all that she had worked for? The two things even to Josie did not appear at the time to be compatible.

"You are taking a long time to think about it. I suppose then it means that your answer is no?"

"You forget I am still under contract with the television series once I have shaken off this other infringement that I brought upon myself!"

Gregg looked a little crestfallen but nevertheless shrugged. "Of course I will abide by your decision although I certainly don't want to lose you when we finally dock back in the U.K!"

"Hardly that. Actually I think the set is contemplating moving up to Salford Quays with a lot of other departments and that is in the North of England!" She tried to sound a little blasé. Not that she felt that way in her heart. "So if you take the job there is no reason why we should lose touch!" To lose touch with this guy would be her worst nightmare. Damn it she loved him, she was prepared to spend the rest of her life with him and yet he did not appear prepared to make that final commitment.

"It's something I will have to think about!" The joviality of earlier on that day when they had been choosing costumes for that night had now all disappeared and as if to give credence to that Gregg picked up a newspaper that was lying on the table where someone had left it.

The rest of the day seemed to pass in the same way and Josie became more and more convinced that the relationship between them had somehow diminished even though politeness prevailed. Perhaps that was the reason why she went to her cabin early to prepare for the evening meal. It was whilst she was in the process of doing this that she spotted Helmut still engrossed with his books in the library. For a moment she felt tempted to stop and have a word with him and apologise for her earlier behaviour but the thought of what Gregg would have said if she had done this stopped her. She even imagined his "Oh let the man be. Perhaps in this sort of mood he's bound to prove a wet blanket!"

The thought stayed with her and she wondered whether she was also acting like a wet blanket with her own current state of mind. That was when she decided to try to forget what had passed between them and concentrate instead on dressing for that evening.

Maybe she was right to do this for the sight of them in their British gear helped to bring a titter to both of their lips as they entered the Restaurant together Even so Helmut obviously chose not to eat with them in the Restaurant for either lunch nor dinner that day and it was much to Josie's surprise that Fern actually decided to join them in the evening, for in truth they had seen little of her in recent days apart that was from those occasions on shore that had been anything if not suspicious. But tonight the girl appeared as large as life making profound apologies for her recent absences but never mentioning anything about what she had being doing during this time. Nor had she dressed for this particular occasion. Indeed she looked around at the others present in the Restaurant as if something had happened that she was totally unaware of. Indeed the girl went as far as to mention the matter and once she was advised of the nature of that evening she claimed that she must have forgotten as she was currently in the process of finalising her work for the art exhibition due to take place in the next couple of days.

For his part Gregg took it upon himself to cast a look in Josie's direction as if he was warning her not to give any inkling of what they themselves had witnessed whilst they had been out and about and indeed he opened the conversation by questioning her attire for that evening.

"So you are not au fait with the British night I take it?"

The other shrugged her shoulders. She had obviously forgotten what she had said earlier. "To me it seems rightly or wrongly to be a complete waste of time. Whether you consider that not to be au fait is your judgement but myself I think the whole thing is really rather silly!" Gregg groaned at her words and glanced at Josie wondering if they had acquired another Helmut

"Sometimes people enjoy being silly as you put it just for sheer enjoyment!"

"Then no doubt they are allowed to voice their own opinion on the matter just so long as I am not involved!"

So this was to be the prevailing atmosphere throughout the meal? Josie began to feel a little sorry that she had attended but Fern's next words served to stop her in her tracks.

"Of course before I go any further I think that apologies are due to you Josie. You see I was so involved with my art classes that I totally forget my promise to you to take you to visit the Pyramids whilst we were on Tenerife. Tell me did you manage to get there after all?" The girl gushed, her conscience perhaps now troubling her just a little. " In fact I seem to have been so tied up with my art work to the exclusion of everything else; sketches and the like that I hope to develop further when I get home although I have been cajoled to exhibit some of my work in the art exhibition of the class's work that is due the day after tomorrow!"

"We will look forward to seeing them!" Josie surprised herself that the words came so easily to her lips.

"You said that you wanted to develop some of your ideas when you got home but then we haven't a clue where your home is?" Gregg put the question in the most plausible terms of enquiry.

"A little place in Northern France. Oh make no mistake I am English only my family uprooted to that region ages ago and we have stayed ever since!"

"Fern has been telling us all about the Canaria Pine that apparently can withstand fire if its interior structure is preserved!" That was when Josie glanced up to see that Helmut had decided to join them after all and it was Helmut moreover who decided now that it was time to add his voice to the proceedings in a rather supercilious fashion or so thought Jose. "Anyway I thought you would like to know that I was in luck for I actually managed to catch the satellite to dispatch my notes to the publisher whilst you were all out!" This was typically Helmut who had now sensed that perhaps as he wasn't the centre of attraction at the time he had better do something to correct the matter, which was possibly the reason why he had decided to join them after all! But then one had to consider that here was a man who up until the present time had never completely grown up and was now exhibiting this self same trend. "Anyway if you do happen to be interested there is a copy for you to peruse in the cabin Gregg!"

Gregg grimaced in Josie's direction for this was not an agenda that was currently occupying his mind and the thought of spending more time in perusing the mass of figures he had already previously looked through back in the cabin was the last thing he wanted to do at that time.

Nevertheless he glanced at Josie almost apologetically as if this was some sort of a bind that he could not escape from.

"Guess it is something that I have to do unfortunately!" He murmured in her direction. "Anyway I promise you it won't take me very long, only long enough to prevent the man from having a fit of the sulks. Still whilst I am attending to that why don't you go along and stake our place upstairs in the lounge for it is bound to get busy up there tonight and I'll join you there as soon as possible?"

Fern looked vaguely interested in what was going on but then shrugged the matter off acting as if she had better things to involve herself in and Josie conceded that as Gregg was probably right and it would probably get busy in the Neptune that night this was possibly the best solution as she forced herself, practically against her will, to remember that Gregg had after all come here with Helmut in the first place and therefore it was perhaps only right that the other would cleave some attention.

The British night on board that vessel was possibly celebrated for all the wrong reasons if one paid any attention to the puritanical strand of thought, but nevertheless it was well supported and therefore it came as little surprise to Josie to consequently meet the tumult of folk moving from point A to point B at the same time, all it appeared now searching for a table and therefore she decided that Gregg had been quite right in insisting that she should go there before him. What he had not visualised however was that on her own as her eyes sought out a vacant table she was to suddenly find herself in the company of Paul Butler who tonight attempted to ooze forth his most charming of manners. An affected act, she swore under her breath as she looked for a way out of the situation for to tell the truth this meeting achieved little for her equilibrium.

"So I take it that you have come to enjoy the show Miss Craven!" He glanced up almost disapprovingly to where the flags now decorated the ballroom and possibly signified that this was really not his scene at all!

"Thank you yes, but if you will excuse me I need to find a table!" She tried her best to get away from this man but he stayed her with his hand.

"As you have left it rather late perhaps you will consider sharing a table with me!" He motioned to an empty place by his side.

"I am expecting Gregg to join me shortly!" It was a flimsy excuse she knew and one that drew an amused expression from the other man his lips twitching in some amusement a she realised something of her discomfort.

"Then I am sure there will be sufficient room for him to sit here as well. No doubt even Gregg will be able to find himself a stool from somewhere when he arrives to join us!" His tone when he mentioned Gregg was condescending but other than standing at the bar and trying to look demure along with a flag that had been thrust into her hand by one of the hosts for the evening she had little option but to take the seat he motioned to and await the further onslaught that she was sure would follow. "I thought that you might like to know that we managed to rectify the mistake you made when you gave your camera to Frederick Hauser yesterday. I have the object here to return to you for I am sure you would not like to lose your holiday snaps. Yes we managed to retrieve the camera Miss Craven although having said that I think that I must complement you on the snaps you took of Miss Astor in the Caldera. A copy of them will prove to be very useful to us especially once they had been enlarged. For then it was possible for us to see not only the Euros in the envelope that you first suspected Fern received at that place but the finer details of the papers which she passed to the person she met there were also quite significant!" He toyed with the camera in question before finally laying it down on the table in front of them. Then glancing at her expression he added with a tinge of sarcasm. "You needn't worry for I can assure you that the holiday snaps you have taken are perfectly safe!"

"I'm afraid that I don't understand! How on earth did you manage to retrieve the camera when we have been at sea after I left it with Frederick on shore?" Even though she was interested in what the envelope Fern had passed to the man contained she still eyed the camera he had now placed on the table almost with some suspicion.

"Oh we arranged for it to be dropped by carrier pigeon!" The man was blasé about the matter and obviously did not wish to confide in her the true method that had been employed to secure the item. Then viewing the incredulous look she gave him. "No in truth one cannot expect you to understand the workings of the Service, but there again one could put that down to your own inexperience in this field. Nevertheless I must still compliment you on the action you took on La Palma even if you did appear to be careless with your findings!"

"In which case it appears that I must have done something right after all!" Her tone was clipped. In all truth she still didn't understand what had happened, nor in actual fact did she care anymore for she now had the distinct desire to get away from this man and quickly.

"Perhaps after all we rather got off on the wrong foot to start with Miss Craven and now maybe we ought to try to rectify the situation by you dancing with me if one can possibly hear the music over this rumpus of noise around us!" He now referred to the background singing of national songs that was still continuing even though the orchestra had started to play something entirely different.

There seemed to be no way she could escape from the vivid eyes that met her own and still against her will Josie now found herself being propelled across the floor by the man she could never deem to be trustworthy. She supposed now his chat appeared to be friendly enough although at the time Josie paid little interest in what he was saying for her eyes searched the crowd for any sign of Gregg. It was whilst she was doing this that she spotted Fern who was to all intents and purposes now frowning in her direction perhaps because she now considered Jose to have laid claim to her own partner.

"I believe Miss Astor is currently looking for you!" At least she did her best to break with the flow of rhetoric he was currently issuing forth.

"No doubt the woman will be patient enough to wait!" His tone suddenly appeared cold almost dismissive as if now he had achieved what he had set out to acquire he had no more time for this girl. This was something that made Josie wonder what Paul Butler now wanted from her for he appeared to have little intention of letting her go a factor made more obvious when the music stopped and he tried to steal his arm around her shoulders whilst for her part Josie tried her best to move away from him. Fate however decreed otherwise for the band had started up yet again and she felt an unwilling participant as her escort persuaded her back onto the floor.

"Surely you were not contemplating leaving so soon Miss Craven?" His voice attempted to exact charm and Josie was reminded of a slithering snake almost ready to pounce.

"I was wondering what had happened to my friend!" Her voice was faltering as she tried to make her excuses.

"You are no doubt speaking of Gregg? But surely he will come and find us in here. After all the boat is not such a large place and to leave now would mean that you would miss the show as well as debarring me from your delightful company. I had not realised before that your social prowess extended to dancing as well as acting!"

Worse was to follow however for as they moved around with Josie still determined not to listen to her escort's chatter, she happened to glance across the lounge only to see Gregg watching the scene with a very puzzled expression on his face. And by the time the music finally stopped and Jose made her excuse to make a quick exit there was now no sign of this man for having watched her on the dance floor the one whom she desired had now apparently left without her!

The union flags were still fluttering when she finally made good her escape, not that Paul Butler had been a particularly easy person to escape from. But seeing Gregg's reaction she was now determined to depart and thus all thoughts of watching the show that was scheduled to follow the dancing was now forgotten, her main intention now to find the one who had apparently taken offence at seeing her with another.

Yet even if the ship was not a large one by the standards of some ocean cruisers there was now no sign of the one whom she sought and she wondered exactly where the man could had chosen to secrete himself at this time. Stepping outside onto the deck to see if she could spot Gregg there she noticed that now even the weather appeared to have changed and the memories of the mysterious Fogo and the fire it issued forth had now faded into complete insignificance. As far as her assignment was concerned she was still confused and she was even more confused in relation to her standing with Gregg and why he had taken affront at her presence with Paul Butler, an inflicted presence that had been none of her doing and something that she believed the man would have realised if indeed the trust that they had established had been something that was permanent!

Still feeling disheartened at not being able to find him Josie finally returned to her cabin, for no longer did the diversions of the night life appeal to her and upon entering even her cabin evoked memories of the previous night that she had shared with Gregg in this very same place where she imagined even some of his odour would have been left on the bedding. It was only then that she remembered that she had left the camera on the table in the Neptune Lounge where Paul had placed it after all. Still there was literally no way that she was for returning to that place in order to collect it, at least not at this moment in time.

It was as she opened the cabin door however that she first noticed the envelope that had been pushed underneath it and rescuing it from the floor she spotted that it was an E Mail.

Short and very much to the point it was from the television company who had employed her now demanding to know when they could expect her back, for to leave the series for much longer would have a detrimental effect on the audience ratings and consequently they felt that they now had the right to know when to write her back into the script. She paused as she scanned the text for a second time. The ship had one more port of call at Lisbon before heading back to the U.K. and therefore she pondered that perhaps the time was right for her to reach some decision over her future. It was something that until today she had not wanted to think about for she had joined this elite Ministry whilst she had taken extended leave to avenge her father's death. It had appeared to be a simple enough option at the time but now everything appeared to have become pear shaped and she now no longer trusted her own judgement on any of this. She remembered her decision of earlier that day. Perhaps indeed it was time for her to seize the initiative and resign from this post and allow someone far more capable than herself to take over the mantle of responsibility for after all acting had been her first love and to be completely parted from it would be a wrench that would sever her body apart.

She remembered back to what Helmut had said earlier on that evening about the satellite behaving itself at that point of time and without considering the matter any further she scribbled down her response. Moving quickly down to the Main Deck she wondered however if the office on that deck would still be open at this hour. Perhaps indeed it was fate that decided that it was just about although in all truth the receptionist looked at her almost disparagingly for leaving it so late to want to send a message that day.

"Surely Madam this item could wait until tomorrow?" The girl was obviously perplexed and perhaps wanted to get away from the office for her own reasons despite having been told to try to always oblige the customers to that place.

"I guess it is rather important!" Surely she hadn't resorted to grovelling. "Plus the fact I did hear from someone that the satellite is reacting well today whilst tomorrow it might well not be the case!"

The girl stared at her for a moment as if she was wondering where she had obtained this information from but then obviously thinking better of her first decision she took the script to return a few minutes later to inform Josie that her message had been dispatched.

Having finally taken this action at last Josie felt that she could relax as she once again thanked the girl who was now at great pains to lock the office door. Yet as far as Josie was concerned she felt that the weight of responsibility had been taken from off her shoulders with her decision made and acted upon. There still appeared to be one more obstacle to overcome however for as she moved away from the office it was to spy Helmut standing in the corridor.

To be fair the man had most probably been studying the shipping charts that were on display there and yet he now appeared both surprised and perhaps a little curious to spot her presence in this place. And Josie silently swore to herself that there was literally no way by which she would divulge her own reasons for going to the office from which he must have spotted her leaving.

"I understood that you were with Gregg?" The question was finally drawn somewhat reluctantly from his lips, his curiosity finally getting the better of him.

"I was, at least I was until he came in search of you because apparently his conscience was troubling him. Since that time I have seen no sign of him!" She bit her lip at the lie she had just told but there was no way she would confess her sighting of him in the Neptune Lounge nor of the way he had turned away when he had spotted her with Paul.

Helmut pulled a face in response. "Well I can assure you that I did not monopolise the man for long. In fact he appeared only too keen to get back to you and enjoy the festivities in the Neptune Lounge!" The man made no effort to disguise the fact that he deplored such a situation which he still considered to be degrading and therefore Josie received renewed input not to expound on the matter.

"In that case I must have missed him somehow, therefore if you will excuse me I will try and make my way back there!" Perhaps if he really thought she was now in the process of going back in search of Gregg he would let her pass. But Helmut for his part now appeared to have no immediate intention of doing that for instead the Marine Biologist had fished in his pocket and suddenly produced a photograph.

"This photograph taken of you at Mindelo Miss Craven, I was under the impression that you had little time for the Baron?"

Josie was mesmerised by the image. Tonight it appeared that photographs were to be the topic of every conversation but this one was different. Indeed the last time she had seen it was when it had been secreted within Fern Astor's art folder and had slipped out onto the floor: A matter that the other person had been quick to rectify at the time. But there was no doubt what the picture portrayed for this was the one that had been taken of her on that Island by Fern herself after Baron Aldermatt had sidled up to her in the grounds of that ranch. Taken at a time when Fern had also been in the company of Paul Butler so that Josie could only hazard a guess at to which of the two of them had instigated it.

The question was however how it had now come into Helmut's possession and her mind could not help but levitate around the notion that this had been Paul Butler's doing, for surely outside of Fern, whom Helmut barely spoke to, Paul Butler seemed to be the one who shared his confidence.

"When one is on an outing such as that one is seldom able to choose one's travelling companions. Whilst it is true that the Baron and I did find ourselves exchanging the time of day I can assure you that there was no way that I sought the man's company on that occasion or come to that on any other. But I am surprised to see such an article in your possession Helmut. After all it hardly serves to stimulate your main interests on this cruise!" Her voice sounded tight for Josie had been compelled to take hold of herself less she took the offending object and tore it up. Yet her mind still focussed on the fact that Helmut now had the article in his possession and the question of how he had managed to come by it remained unanswered.

"I happened to find it amongst the documentation I left in the library!" At least he appeared to want to answer her question. Not that this answer served to satisfy her by any means for the whole scenario appeared to be just a little too contrived. "Therefore as the celluloid contains your features I beg to return it!" He offered it to her and taking hold of the object Josie crushed it up in her hands.

"There was no way I sanctioned the photograph in the first place so perhaps that answers your question Helmut!" Her voice sounded crushed like someone stepping on broken ice but in her heart she wondered if this man had already told Gregg and whether this was the reason why he appeared to have easily taken offence earlier in the evening when she had been dancing with Paul against her will. What was more she still determined that man had some role to play in this. Was he really trying to come between her and Gregg for his own reasons and had found a willing ally in the unsuspecting Helmut? And furthermore how did Fern Astor fir into all this?

"And now if you will excuse me I have just realised that I have other matters to attend to!" At least she prided herself that she still possessed her acting skills as she brushed the Marine Biologist to one side and she just prayed that these well-rehearsed skills would be enough to hide the tumult she now felt in her mind.

Apparently however Helmut had exhausted his say and let her pass and she moved back towards the lift trying to act the part of some dignified person belonging to the noble class.

Not of course that act could be maintained for long and by the time she reached her cabin tears of frustration were already beginning to appear in her eyes and threatened the make up on her face. All she now desired was to be left on her own at peace so that she could refresh her mind after all that had happened. Yet the impending solitude did little to soothe her and if she for one moment had secretly hoped that Gregg would come to find her and they could talk these matters through, then she was to be very much disappointed.

Perhaps indeed the knock on the door sometime later served to give her false hope, maybe she had been wrong in her thinking and her lover had come after all to find her, but even as she eagerly opened the obstacle that prevented her from seeing who was there it was to find the cabin steward who was now stood outside with something in his hand.

"I believe you left your camera behind on the table in the Neptune Lounge Madam. I was asked to return it to you!"

The object appeared tainted when she took it off the young man even though she was still surprised to receive it and after the steward departed she felt compelled to view the aperture to see whether her snaps were indeed intact. They were and she paused again when she came to the snaps of Fern that had been taken at the Caldera and wondered what those enlargements that both Frederick and Paul in their turn had been on about had really shown up. Of course she had at the time no way of knowing of the shot taken of the contents of the envelope that Fern had passed to her contact and of the enlargement that showed a sequence of numbers. Indeed even if she had it was quite impossible that she could have discerned what they were about or of the fact that Paul Butler had contacted someone else on the matter that very same evening for Josie was destined to spend a miserable night without her lover to soothe her and still churning over in her mind what had transpired and what indeed Paul Butler's role was in all this. For she did not doubt that the man was implicated!

Chapter Eleven

Josie finally roused from the most fitful of sleeps and remembered that this was the day they were due to reach their last port of call on this cruise. Feeling vaguely uninterested at the thought she would have rolled over to try to make up some of the lost sleep during the night except that the sound of voices in the companionway served to remind her that the time was later than what she had first surmised and therefore with sleep's seal still in her eyes she reached for her watch to find out what the hour was exactly.

She sighed a little dispiritedly when she realised that it was time for her to think of easing her frame from that bunk but then she supposed that was what lack of sleep did for a person, one was unable to obtain proper rest during the night but come the morning all one wanted to do was to climb back into bed!

Her eyes focussed on the door to her cabin and for the first time she realised that something had been pushed underneath it in the silence of the night for she had heard no one approach her abode even though her sleep for what it was, had been but light and patchy. After eyeing the paper that had been placed there for several more minutes, and after realising that lying in the prone position she was unlikely to find out what it was all about, she finally forced her frame from off the mattress in order to pick it up, firmly believing as she did so that this must be a summary of her shipboard account for such an item was due to be delivered to the cabin that day.

The fact that it was not as she had expected, possibly assisted in opening her eyes more fully and consequently forcing the grains of unused sleep from out of their illicit corners. Instead of the shipboard account the paper contained a message that had obviously been received by telephone in the office and it merely stated that Frederick wished to see her later on that morning at an appointed spot on shore. No details as to why were given but the reason for this she supposed was pretty obvious as she forced herself into the shower in an attempt to wash away the remaining particles of the night. No doubt the man had still something that he wished her to accomplish. The thought of the camera, not to mention its mysterious return, did occur to her but she discounted the matter for surely Frederick would be the one who was able to provide the explanation of how it had arrived back on board as well as supplying the answer to several other matters that she felt now needed to be cleared in her mind. Still one thing seemed to be in her favour as she finally glanced at her watch and found that she was relieved to see that she hadn't overslept after all and consequently she had therefore ample time to make this rendezvous without her initial feeling that somehow she had woken late.

Still Lisbon, their last port of call, was to prove no different to any other city when it rained, and rain it did on the morning of their arrival. Josie decided that if she had been like many of the others on the cruise she might well have declined leaving the ship, for in fact many of the ones who had not already booked to go on excursions at this place decided to do exactly that. But then as far as Josie was concerned things appeared to be a little different especially after she had received Frederick's message that he needed to see her and she had been directed to meet him in the square where the yellow trams crossed over before they veered at one side up the hill that led to the castle.

The meeting was scheduled for eleven o'clock and getting to this place presented little problem for her as a shuttle bus from the port had been provided and moreover with the current prevailing weather conditions and folk consequently declining to leave the ship there would consequently be no great demand for places on it and therefore no gauntlet to run.

She had seen no sign of Gregg again that morning, which was a factor much to her dismay, for the man had not been in the Restaurant and when approached Helmut had simply shook his head and deliberately declined to throw any light on the fellow's absence. Neither upon her arrival in the restaurant had there been signs either of the other two although Helmut did arrive just as she was about ready to leave. To do him justice Helmut tried at the time to draw her into polite conversation but chattering with this fellow was not exactly what Josie had in mind for in truth she was still feeling pangs of guilt after the previous evening for Gregg's expression upon spotting her with Paul remained still fresh in her mind, but on the other hand she supposed on reflection that as she herself had sought to have her breakfast at the first opportunity on that day so that she would be in time to catch the first shuttle to this place that had been destroyed by an earthquake in 1785, then it was possible she had missed him not by any designed strategy but simply on a question of her timing.

Even so such feelings of guilt, she told herself, was a matter that she now had to attend to completely on her own and moreover, shake off the lethargy that she was currently experiencing, for she had not been the one responsible for the misunderstanding that had occurred between the two of them the previous evening. The blame if any was to be apportioned, must be laid squarely at the feet of Paul Butler for surely he had been the one who had been solely responsible. And the thought of Paul Butler now made her more determined than ever to carry out this assignation for Frederick in a way had already intimated that the Department was now becoming a little impatient at her lack of success in the quest they had required of her. What was more to the point Frederick in his note had also intimated that Paul Butler had previously been sighted in this part of the metropolis, and perhaps more than ever this was the knowledge had helped to spur her on, so determined she was to gain anything she could against the man, whom to her mind was the one who must have been responsible for that photograph falling into Helmut's hands, who hoping perhaps to extend the rift between Gregg and herself would surely have informed him of the photo's contents.

Gritting her teeth at such thoughts she had left the dining table to return to her cabin to collect her bag before she made for the gangway. Once there at any other time she might well have interpreted the gaze she received from the security personnel who swiped her card as she left the ship to go ashore as being something that was a little unusual. But even so she would not have known about the phone call that this same man charged with security had made as her feet negotiated the gangplank, which because of the tide flow made things even more difficult to negotiate. Not that she should have experienced any problems for getting on and off boats seemed to have become a way of life lately. A lifestyle that the presenter of the film set was currently persuading her to hurry up and change. But that would shortly be accomplished just as soon as this boat reached British waters again.

It did not take long for shuttle the bus that had been provided to reach the city centre and very soon she found that she was leaving it to step into a mass of towering buildings. She felt fortunate that Frederick was there waiting for her at the place he had stipulated even though the man appeared to be a little more stern faced than usual.

"Paul Butler has apparently already left the boat before you. I spotted him crossing over Praca de Comerdo Square a short time ago. Therefore if you keep to this main thoroughfare where the fashionable shops are you ought to be able to catch him up possibly just past the Elevator de Santa Justa!"

It never occurred to her to question how Paul had managed to achieve this feat considering that she was the one who had caught the first shuttle bus and he had not been on it, or why Frederick, if the Service currently employed him, had bothered to involve her in this instead of seeing to the matter for himself, or indeed why he foresaw the necessity for catching up with Paul Butler for any reason! Indeed whether such matters involved the application of certain talents solely to the task allotted was a point upon which she had yet to decide. Neither was Frederick any more forthcoming as to why he had wanted to see her this morning. But then she supposed that he had after all been of great assistance to her in the past and therefore she felt no reason to argue against his motives.

Perhaps Frederick realised something of her present mood for he suddenly smiled wryly in her direction. "Sorry but I guess I have to leave you here on your own after all as other matters are now pressing on my time, but this is the place where you can catch the bus back to the ship later on. Remember however that the last shuttle is scheduled for five o'clock, so good luck on your venture. Remember all that you are expected to do is to follow the man and find out what he is currently up to, who he meets if anyone and then report back!"

She watched perhaps a little dumbfounded at this proposed change in events as he left her before she commenced to walk up the street where the gutters were already filling up with water and she fished in her bag to retrieve an umbrella before it occurred to her to query what this venture was supposed to be. But by this time and despite the rain the place was beginning to throb with local commuters and therefore there seemed little else she could do but intermingle with them, follow the instructions that had been given to her and keep her eyes open all the time for the man whom she sought. Even so she still had many streets to cross before she arrived at the places mentioned and passing those yellow trams of yesteryear again as they travelled up to the Castle suddenly put her in mind of Baron Aldermatt and his own domain. Maybe in her own mind castles always appeared to have a sinister spectre attached to them and she supposed as far as she was concerned one such sinister spectre could be said to be the Baron himself!

She smiled at her vivid imagination as she waited for the traffic lights to change and at the same time she managed to miss spotting the character whom she had sought, the person who was currently stood in a shop doorway behaving as if he himself was on the look out for someone. It was only after she had passed this person by that she realised that someone was currently close behind her and after being told of the plague of pickpockets that frequented the squares and other places of interest to the visitor in that city she made to draw her own bag more tightly around her.

Yet the person who was following her now appeared to get closer however: In desperation she tried to quicken her step but even as she did so she felt the brunt of something poking in her back and the sound of a muffled voice hissing the orders over her shoulder. "You will take the next turning on the right. If you value your life I would advise you to keep on walking and not to stop or turn round!"

At one time in her life Josie would have objected to obeying such orders. For starters she was certain that her namesake Kimberley Clark would have taken some action if this had happened to her, but now and more especially after the lack of sleep the previous night, she felt exhausted and it seemed easier to obey than to argue with the fiend who was presently still poking some object that she believed to be some sort of weapon into the small of her back. At the top of this street up yet another climb she noticed that there was a door leading from the street. Yet before she had time to puzzle out where this led to, she found herself forced to open it and to enter. Thus passing through an archway it was to suddenly find herself surprisingly enough in a garden of flowers. Such a sight of beauty in the midst of this city and diametrically opposed to the stifling air of the Metro or even her current situation gave Josie quite a surprise. So much so that as conscious as she was of the figure behind her she did not immediately spot a further person who was currently sat down on a form at the far end of this oasis. That was however until this person stood with his enormous body towering over her own.

"So we meet again Miss Craven!" Her surprise was all the greater for this person had obviously been expecting her. "Still before you recover from your obvious surprise at seeing me again perhaps we ought to discuss our business. As I am under the impression that there are currently certain things in your possession that I now desire, shall we start with the map you have first of all?"

"I am afraid that I have no idea what you are talking about?" She looked up into the face of Baron Aldermatt whilst still fighting hard to feign her innocence and it had to be said that in spite of her current situation she was compelled to compliment herself on her acting ability.

"But I on the other hand feel quite sure that you do my dear. I believe that it was passed onto you as one of your father's effects. I believe I am correct in saying that, am I not Frederick?"

Josie swallowed hard as she realised that the man who had held something in her back and forced her into this place had been Frederick Hauser. The whole matter was incomprehensible and yet the why's had to be forced to wait until later as she steeled herself to reply.

"I am afraid that I possess no map of any description apart that is from a certain street map of this city that I was handed when I came here on the bus!" Perhaps for the first time Josie felt glad that she had left the blasted map with Helmut as she saw Frederick now fidgeting behind her and wondered what the hell this man was playing at.

"I am afraid that my informant has already told me differently. There is also the question of a camera that you managed to take some photographs with. Where does that happen to be at the present time for you do not appear to have come prepared to take photographs in Lisbon, a matter that I find most unusual in a tourist? And yet I was informed that the object had already been returned to you against my precise instructions!"

He had spoken of his informant and her camera! Her eyes spun round onto Frederick for surely he was the only person in this place who had known of such things. The Baron followed her gaze. "You have done well Frederick, you have nothing to reprove yourself of even if the young lady is not for telling us willingly. But perhaps I can refresh your memory my dear. The map that was in your possession, well I now require it. Your camera on the other hand has certain snaps contained on the disk that we would not like to fall into the wrong hands. Therefore as we are well aware that you have currently access to both of these objects perhaps you will now make both items available to us and this matter need go no further!"

"Never!" The word sounded far braver than the way she currently felt as her mind propelled itself around in circles trying to establish the logic of this meeting.

"You do not take the opportunity to make things easy for yourself I note. Very well then we will be forced to resort to other means!" He shouted to someone who appeared from out of a side door and Josie gulped as she saw the artist appear on the scene but now the friendly features that this girl had once exhibited had all disappeared. "Perhaps you should start by searching the girl Fern, after all it is through your carelessness that Miss Craven found evidence to indict you! A matter I might add that is now proving to be a great inconvenience to me!"

All Josie could now think of as the girl snatched her bag to empty it and later moved to search her pockets was why Frederick did not intervene but the man stood passively by whilst all this happened and did not say a word. Indeed he seemed to be more intent on toying with the weapon he had held than eyeing her present predicament! The only thing that Josie was now relieved about was that she had finally parted with the gun, for lethal or otherwise if they had found it on her the consequences might have been different.

"You appear to have been correct in what you initially told us Miss Craven. Therefore I suggest that if you do wish to catch your cruise boat before it leaves you will tell Fern and Frederick here exactly where they will find the objects when they return to the boat. And of course you will stay here as my guest until they return. If they do not find what they seek then I do not think the British Government will shed too many tears over losing one co-opted agent. Your only solution is therefore to tell us what we wish to know!"

"I think not!" She hadn't heard the door open or Paul Butler step over the threshold. Indeed at first she failed to recognise his voice. "I guess Josie will be coming with me!" He waved a gun in his hand first of all at the unfortunate Frederick who hastened to drop his own weapon and then at the rest of the gathering. "Right Josie shall we move now!"

He waved to her to get outside and Josie did not hesitate to do his bidding before he floored Frederick with a glancing blow and then succeeded in fastening the outside door firmly shut behind them. There was a quick telephone call before he spoke again. "Right, we move now, we need to get back to the boat before these have the wit to follow! That is unless the police whom I have just summoned arrive here first!" Where that tandem had come from that he had waiting outside she dared not hazard a guess. All she knew was that the next moment she was pedalling furiously with him back in the direction of the port. "We talk only once we are back on board ship!" His orders were quite clear and precise now and Josie was not in any mood for argument at that time!

"I guess that was a close call!" He finally spoke once they had cleared the gangplank and security. "But I doubt if any of them will take the chance to follow us here. Still what the hell made you go ashore on your own in the first place?"

"I had a message to meet Frederick!" Someone had once said that confession was good for the soul and she still could not understand what role this man had been playing in the shindig that had just ensued.

"And of course you went without question like some innocent babe to the slaughter?"

"At the time it seemed reasonable enough to me for after all Frederick Hauser has been more of a friend to me in the past!"

"I presume you mean by that he has appeared to be more of a friend to you than what I have been? That if I might be so bold as to say so was a well-acted performance, perhaps indeed worthy of your own stage efforts. He may not have killed your father Josie but he did kill the initial contact, the person who was supposed to meet you at Koblenz. He killed the man for his own reasons, which I might add were mainly to ingratiate himself firmly in your mind so that you felt that you could trust him for even at that time we were well aware of exactly where you would end up. Not that I didn't for my part argue with the relevant authorities for employing you in the first place for believe you me this is no job for a mere novice even if she can employ some good acting skills, but they for their part had decided that employing a female would prove less conspicuous in infiltrating certain company. Anyway looking at your face one would suggest that you are in need of a stiff drink therefore shall we continue this conversation in the bar instead of blocking up the passageway?"

She supposed that she must have followed him like some puppy dog anxious to learn more for the whole experience was still shaking her self-confidence. Not that Paul seemed to notice anything amiss as he marshalled her to the bar and placed a large brandy in front of her. "Anyway to return to what we were talking about when we were making a damned nuisance of ourselves blocking off the deck space for the people returning to the ship, I did actually worry as to how you would cope. That was why I finally persuaded our mutual employers to allow me to take up Helmut's kind offer of assisting him on this diving exploit for in spite of Gregg the two of us go back a long way. The idea was initially to keep a watchful eye over you, a factor that you immediately appeared to resent. Why was that? Did you still believe that I was the one responsible for killing your father?"

She took a long sip of her brandy before she nodded in response. "I'm afraid that I did!"

"Then it would appear that those in charge did a good job in convincing you in that matter although in all truth it is just as well the authorities gave you a faulty weapon otherwise I might not have been available to come to your rescue today!"

"But I thought that you and Fern -----?"

"Had taken up together, is that what you really thought? You still have a great deal to learn as to how the Service operates. Fern was a suspect even before we left because of her relationship with some of the French officials at the time when the news was released about our two countries sharing certain defensive strategies. But Fern the artist did not stop there in her relationships with other powers and she used her artistic prowess to good effect in that field. Yet whilst she played a clever game in disguising the common ground held between herself and Frederick Hauser she could not help but crow at her attachment to the Baron who also carried with him a wave of suspicion, something that was initially reported to headquarters by your own father. For the Baron is reputed to have Middle Eastern contacts of which possibly enough has already been said!"

"Yet all the time you allowed me to think----------!"

"That I was the one who was in league with the disreputable man? Yes, you made that quite obvious to me Josie. But then that is probably what divides us for you have no idea of the true mythology of the Service and how it actually functions. That was the reason I cried against you ever being appointed to this task and now my advice to you is to leave the Service as soon as it is possible and return to your acting profession in which you are good. That way you will be able to avoid asking too many pertinent questions that I will be unable to answer!"

"There is still one thing that puzzles me. How on earth did you manage to get that camera back when we were at sea?"

"You really do persist in asking far too many questions but for what it is worth we have Helmut to thank for that. I told you that he was a friend and the one thing we required was to get hold of those damning snaps that indicted Fern Astor and her contacts. Of course at the time you were not even aware that Helmut had been ashore at La Palma nor that he took the opportunity to follow you and oblige me by sneaking the camera away from Frederick when it was least expected, something that I could not have achieved by myself!"

"And the picture that you took of me with the Baron on Mindelo?"

"That was not my doing but rather it was Fern's. She initially took the snap in order to try to implicate you, which is something else that you need to thank Helmut for, as he was the one to retrieve it! But now I have afforded you as many explanations as I am prepared to do for the rest remains a Service matter even if against all odds you have managed to do the Service a favour. I see Gregg has just come into the bar. Perhaps it is time for me to tender my apologies to him for monopolising the girl he obviously prefers to be with. It will be a tale that no doubt he will find the greatest difficulty in understanding, but something that needs to be said!"

She glanced at Paul still unable to believe that this one had acted as her saviour that day. After his behaviour the previous evening she would have found it easy to ignore Gregg but then Paul would hear nothing of it.

"Perhaps you had better sit down. But first can I get you a drink?" The offer was there but Gregg rapidly shunned the idea.

"As a diver I never partake in any alcoholic substance during the day. As you also happen to be a diver perhaps that is something that you too would be wise to observe!"

"Then please sit down and take the weight off your feet for this is a long story and something that I am determined you must hear!"

Now Gregg sat down with a shrug but without further questioning although his eyes still refused to meet those of Josie. Neither could it be said that Paul spared any punches in the telling of the saga. There was a silence when he finished finally to be broken by Gregg. "So you are asking me to believe that your sole purpose for being here was to keep a watchful eye on Josie?"

"That was my main initial intention yes although I still feel she is vastly unsuited in the role she has adopted!"

"And what role is that exactly?"

"Stop it the pair of you!" Josie had heard enough. "Maybe I have some news for both of you. As I am obviously of no use to the Service as Paul here keeps insisting is the truth I would now like the pair of you to know that I have now resigned, they can have their shilling back or whatever it takes to convince them that I mean exactly what I say. Furthermore I have also responded to an E Mail that requested me to return to the television series and moreover I have now told them that I fully intend to resume my character just as soon as this boat is back in the U.K. Therefore if the Ministry or anyone else does not like my decision then I am afraid that it is tough for I have already made it and also acted upon it!"

A silence ensued following her delivery and that was when Josie grasped the opportunity to stand and to walk away. As far as she was concerned the two of them could go to hell, she had just about heard enough. Now she determined it would be cabin service for her for the rest of the time on board. That way she could avoid meeting the lot of them! The irony of the situation was that as she passed by the Main Deck the art exhibits of the class on board were now on public view with Fern's occupying pride of place!

It was a calm sea when they finally approached the shores of the U.K and certainly not as they had previously feared for during their absence the storms had wrecked the coastlines practically in every part of the country. It was with some thought that Josie dutifully packed her case ready for collection outside of her cabin. She expected that once they docked there would be some sort of special car waiting for her to whisk her away for a debriefing session, for the ones in grey suits would never credit the fact that her life in the Service was over. She even imagined their voices ricocheting around the walls of that sombre building, "I'm afraid that you cannot do that. Once employed in the Service people do not wish to opt out in such a manner. Besides remember all the expense you have cost us in these days of austerity. No, we consider that you are not thinking correctly. Perhaps you are in need of a rest period!"

Still perhaps what was bugging her even more than the thought of those voices was that the symbolic symbol of the car would be responsible for whisking her out of Gregg's life for she doubted whether the Service would approve of her having a Marine Biologist for a boy friend. And then she suddenly bethought herself for the relationship she had held with Gregg was now well and truly over, she had not seen him since that time in the bar when she had walked off. He had never tried to call her on the internal telephone, nor had he been around to knock on her cabin door. Therefore to her mind the relationship that they once held dear must have finally reached a conclusion.

Still she supposed that she still had her role as Kimberley Clark to go back to. After all she had been happy there hadn't she? Feelings of self-doubt however still accosted her feelings. Whilst her father had been alive she supposed that she had always considered acting as a way of escapism from many of the strictures he had placed on her early life, for once lost in the part she could easily immerse herself into a land of make belief.

Suddenly there was a tap on the cabin door and Josie stopped what she was doing. The female steward responsible for her cabin was the only one who would enter without receiving acknowledgement believing her to be out at the time, but Grace had already completed her rounds for that morning giving Josie a knowing smile as she had passed by. She heard a voice now calling out to her but again Josie remained silent. She recognised the voice but after all that had happened she now felt too reticent to respond.

The voice called out again to her this time louder than before. "Come on and open this door Josie. I know full well that you are still in there for Grace said as much. Open this door now or I swear that I'll have everyone out of their cabins wondering what all the fuss is about!"

Josie never for a moment doubted that Gregg was well capable of doing that and consequently she opened it half an inch or so but not wide enough for the man to get his foot in. Perhaps however in her hurry to accomplish that she underestimated his resilience for once his fingers had managed to prise themselves round the side of that door he wrest it from her grasp and she stepped back as he deliberately entered the cabin uninvited.

"Perhaps you will be good enough to explain to me what the hell you think that you are playing at?" His voice now practically rasped at her but with the cabin door now firmly in his control he also deliberately made to close it behind his form.

"I was simply packing up. It is a requirement if you remember for our cases have to be outside before bedtime tonight!"

"And you have needed to spend the last twenty four hours packing it? Come off it Josie I think I know you better than that!"

"If you must know I decided that perhaps I was better off here than sitting listening to myself being berated by the pair of you!" Maybe something of her Irish temperament was beginning to manifest itself. Even so she underestimated the attraction that such a fiery glow now gave her

"Berated! Is that what you call Paul's attempt to put me in the picture as to what has been happening? Did it never occur to you that the man was exonerating himself for seemingly having monopolised you of late, because he wanted no misunderstanding on my part? Did it never occur to you that the man probably saved your life back in Lisbon as well as your pitiful career in your so called Service?"

Josie swallowed hard. "All that hardly matters now for you see I have already decided to return to my role as Kimberley Clark and therefore I thought I had already made it quite clear that as far as I am concerned the Service can have their so called career!"

"And you think you will be able to get away from them quite so easily?"

"Of course, I have already made up my mind!"

"And what about making up your mind concerning other matters. Would you have left the Service for me Josie?"

"For you?"

"Yes for me damn it! Don't you realise woman that I want to marry you whether the Service like it or not?"

"You want to marry me?"

"Yes damn it I do! Surely you realised what I thought about you, why, haven't we already spoken of the future together? O.K. I admit I portrayed a jealous streak when

Paul Butler appeared to be muscling his way in, I admit for what it is worth that I was jealous, and now I am sorry for it but it is still no excuse for you locking yourself away in this cabin!"

"What did you expect me to do then? You mentioned nothing of marriage before!" The words were out before she realised that she had spoken

"But I thought you understood my intentions!" The man looked perplexed. "It was you who never responded to my suggestion of applying for that job in the North of England. I knew damned well that your set was being moved to Salford Quays. It's common knowledge if one reads the papers and I also knew that you would probably want to return there at least for a time until you find that you have other commitments. Therefore my idea was that until that time came we could both commute when necessary!"

"You had worked all that out without telling me?"

"You forget I was waiting for your answer Josie and I must confess you have the knack of making a man go through hell whilst he is waiting!"

"Then I apologise if that is what you think!"

"In that case can I take it that you will marry me after all?"

"If that is what you want!"

"This is what I want!" Gregg made no further bones but grabbed hold of her forcing his lips onto her own. It was a long time before she found the breath to speak but finally wresting her head from beneath his own she managed to gasp out her response with all the breath that she could muster.

"O.K then I will marry you that is what I want!"

The war of words finally over the victor gave a whoop of delight as he kissed her again more tenderly this time around.

"So what do you suggest we do now?" She eyed him through the eyes that finally confessed the love that she felt for him.

"Do? You of all people asking a question like that! Why I consider that we should spend our last night on board out of this cabin, at least for part of it and announce to all who are willing to listen that we can now be considered to be an item and after that we will return here and I will try to tell you just how much you really mean to me!"

"But what of Helmut? It appears that I owe him a debt of gratitude!"

"Helmut will have to be satisfied in your decision that maybe you will occasionally allow me to dive with him. The man already knows how I feel about you. A factor that he accepts although he swears that if he lives to be a hundred he will never understand the mentality of the English. But I have not come here to talk about Helmut for I believe we have far more interesting matters to discuss; that is of course once I have satisfied myself that you truly love me!"

"And you still have doubts on that?"

"I have until you prove me wrong and you can start doing that right here and now!" The look in his eyes now gave her all the reassurance that she required as once again his arms enfolded her and they were lost in the passion of the ages!

★ ★ ★ ★

Agent for love.

duet for male and female voice

With feeling
Tempo: 80

Words and Music by J.Steele
Contact 01253 591905

If I told you that I loved you, what would you do? Then I gent- ly kissed your lips just so. How would you feel if I be- gan to car- ess you?

I am sinc- ere and I want to know!

Verse3

If I was an artist I'd show you my etchings

Offer to paint you in poses you choose,

Arrange your posture - make many sketchings,

Whilst you relax and peruse.

Verse5

We must live every second of life

However long that may be.

If I asked you to be my wife

What would you say to me?

Agent for love. (duet)

female part

With feeling
Tempo: 80

afl2

Words and Music byJ.Steele
Contact 01253 591905

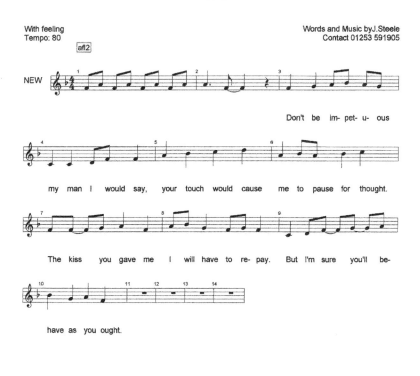

NEW

Don't be im- pet- u- ous

my man I would say, your touch would cause me to pause for thought.

The kiss you gave me I will have to re- pay. But I'm sure you'll be-

have as you ought.

Verse4

My senses are stirring it is a sign

That you are a guy who stands tall.

But if our love is to taste like old wine

We must make haste slowly --that's all!

Verse6

Show me your etchings dear boy

Then kiss me while I'm in this pose

If you turn me on you'll find joy

So don't fail this blossoming rose.

Other Novels By Kathleen Steele

Marina Baixa –

Romance and Intrigue leads from the security of the Lake District to uncertainty in Spain!

Arms Of Gold –

Following September 11th, what connection does the Lake at Windermere have with the Mediterranean around Majorca?

Radiant Vibes –

Pollution in the Irish Sea leads to strange findings and unusual relationships!

Oasis In Time –

The location of those illusive weapons of mass destruction provides surprises!

Put And Take –

Casinos on the Fylde Coast? Would you like to take a chance?

The Upper Cut –

Scurrilous behaviour on those Upper Reaches serves to create ripples that stir those once still waters!

The Pink Rose –

The Border Folk's response to the proposed Regional Assemblies brings mayhem!

Two Faced –

Buying a computer should require a Government Health Warning!

Round And Round –

Wind and Tide can make uneasy bedfellows in the struggle to find a new Power Source!

Next Stop Paradise –

Love and intrigue are stimulated on life's merry-go-round!

Check Out –

The development of the provincial Airport, heralds the development in human relationships

Hide And Seek –

Hidden treasures require attention to detail, or else!

Lost And Found –

Where there's a will, there's a way!

Footloose –

When a positive charge meets a positive charge, then !

In The Shadow Of The Storm –

Do the fish always behave like that or is this the calm before the storm?

Distraction –

A hidden cell in the Lake District leads to a tempest of ferocity which contrasts sharply with the peace and tranquillity that place is noted for!

A Lighter Shade Of Pink –

A sequel as requested to THE PINK ROSE. Meet the various characters again as this time our friends attempt to extend their franchise into

Cumbria!

The Heart's Refrain –

The mists around those magical Islands reflect the mist that obscures Anton's vision.

The Turn Of The Wheel –

Romance and fortune can be linked!

Vengeful Return -

Two men and yet there can only ever be one boat! A sequel to *Marina Baixa* and *Nextstop* Paradise

Not Here -

What is the connection between that house fire and those windmills out at sea?

The Run Of The Rabbit –

Could the government really be conspiring to move that Nuclear Power Plant into the midst of the Langdale Valley?

Star Of The Dawn –

Can the star of early morning point the way to life's fulfilment?

Sketch Me Love –

The shrouding mist of those tranquil Islands serves to disguise a more sinister scheme to involve them in man's game!

Split Wide Open –

Mischievous Pranks or mysterious happenings disturb the peace in the hamlet of FellBeck!

Powerful Circles-

What is the connection between those ancient customs and the future?

Bispham Brook –

Could this be the case where such water comes to create mayhem or is there something more sinister behind the apparently innocent flow?

Crab Island –

The Atlantic Isles offer peace, tranquillity and dramatic scenery to the innocent holidaymaker yet one cannot but speculate that there is something more!

Shap –

The fells of North West England may provide a refuge but other things also transpire in a community that proves that they are not quite so isolated!

Inner Turmoil -

Recovering from a trauma in her life Krisha is soon to find that the past often has a habit of catching up on one!

Crisp Lies The Track –

Will the ashes of the past support the love of today?

The Viper's Bite –

Beware of reptiles with warm blood in their veins!

Softly The Night –

Rags to riches perhaps?

Veil Of Secrets –

Can love survive the tide of deception?

Web Of Torment -

When the storm infiltrates, can peace survive?

Strictures Of The Heart -

Eruption serves to spark the heart.

Echoes From The Past –

Harmony sounds a discordant note.

A Natural Choice –

Water water everywhere, be careful where you step.

If you have difficulty in obtaining any of the above copies contact 01253 591905